Donald McCaig

Milestone Moods and Memories

Poems and Songs

Donald McCaig

Milestone Moods and Memories
Poems and Songs

ISBN/EAN: 9783744772709

Printed in Europe, USA, Canada, Australia, Japan

Cover: Foto ©Andreas Hilbeck / pixelio.de

More available books at **www.hansebooks.com**

MILESTONE MOODS AND MEMORIES.

Poems and Songs.

BY

DONALD McCAIG,

Author of Reply to John Stuart Mill, on the Subjection of Women.

Toronto:
PRINTED BY HUNTER, ROSE & COMPANY.
1894.

PREFACE.

DEAR reader, some of the trifles found on the following pages have lain in my desk for nearly forty years; others of them for over twenty. I am not certain that I can now offer any adequate excuse for the folly of publishing them, but the saddest feeling, and the darkest word written or spoken in any language, is " annihilation." Even to be forgotten amid earthly surroundings is not a pleasant contemplation.

When I sleep, I think I would prefer doing so on some gentle hill, with the maples and pines waving over me, to resting beneath the proudest monument; but in any case I pray that neither warmest friend nor worst enemy will do me the dishonor of placing over me in iron, marble, or brass, " Born May 15th, 1832, died ———." If this be all, not this, for mercy's sake.

Perhaps it is this egotism or vanity, which had haunted me through all the old pioneer days, and has followed me ever since, through all the changes the years have brought, which is now responsible for what, I am aware, can bring me but little fame, and less fortune. All I have ever hoped for in my most sanguine moments has been, that when Canada has outgrown her novitiate, when she has a literature of her own, and a standing among the nations of the earth, I might be recognized as one who had in her then, long ago, seen some beauty in Nature, some grandeur in country and home, some greatness in God, and something of heaven in the face of woman, and had, in some sort worth remembering, recorded his convictions.

Dear reader, this is an open confession. The rest I leave with you.

DONALD McCAIG.

CONTENTS.

MILESTONE MOODS AND MEMORIES.

IN MEMORIAM.

THE shadows lengthen, and the sinking sun
Gilds the far mountain with a golden crest;
The Autumn clouds stretch motionless and dun,
Like cold grey ocean in the distant West.
With sixty years of life gone o'er my head,
I sit and dream of all those years have seen,—
Of the strange paths by which my steps were led,
Up to this hour by hill and valley green,
With varying aims and hopes that erst had been.

The moments vanish, hours unflagging pass,
The days roll on, that measure off our lives;
Youth's pictures tarnish, and the years, alas!
Leave us but little for which manhood strives,—
For all the dreams whereon Ambition fed,
For all the flowers Hope scatter'd by the way,
For all the loves, forgotten, false or dead,
For all the promised fruitage of our May,
How little garner'd at the close of day.

The years go by, with all they had to bring,
The promise, and the pleasure, and the pain,
The longing in the songs we did not sing;
The race in which we cannot run again.
The hills are dim, and far we hoped to climb,
The die is cast, our patrimony spent,
We rest us now on this far brink of Time,
And trifle with the semblance of content:
This only left, of all the gods had sent.

Ah me! we cannot stem the tide of age,
That silent steals in darkness of the night,
Nor pluck one vain regret from memory's page,
Nor change life's written record, dark or bright.
The hills may melt, the mountains may not be,
The world of waters over empires roll,
And hamlets deck the valleys of the sea,
But what shall change the deeply written scroll,
Of three score years imprinted on the soul?

Our treasures linger longest shrined in tears,—
The songs that thrilled our hearts long, long ago.—
The voices now that only fancy hears,—
The hands we cannot clasp again below:
For recreant memory leaves her valued stores
Of fame or riches that have taken wings,
Which once she valued most, now least deplores,—
When the lone heart returns to other things,
O'er which in other days she wept, now lowly sings!

Amid those shadows pale of vanished years,
Seen through the haze that gathers on the hill,—

Gleams of youth's friendships and bereavement's tears;
Dear native land, my thoughts are with thee still;
And though my song must bear a chasten'd strain,
From which all passion has been washed and wrung,
Through glow of joy, or bitter wail of pain,
Or darkest hour that hath been wept or sung,
Turn I to thee, more than when heart was young.

My dear loved land! thou all in all to me,
Of home or country woven through my life,
Till all its texture now is part of thee,
Chased with the flowers of joy, the scars of strife!
In younger days I longed for other climes,
In song or story, more for glory meet.
O Bonny Doon, like far cathedral chimes,
How seemed thy song to me, the sole retreat
Of that strange sorrow of which pain is sweet!

But now I seek no other land afar,
I know no other clime so bright as thee;
What now I am, what we together are,
I must remain, I can no other be;
For I but bear the color, sense and sound,—
The mingled woof and warp of joy and tears,—
The wrong and right of Time's unchanging round,
That stone by stone, to monument it rears,
The all we feel and suffer through the years.

Like echoes come the songs of long ago,
At early morn that through the forest rung;
The little clearing waking in the glow
Of life's brave struggle, when the heart was young.

In soft, low murmurs steal across the vale,
The notes of labor failing, as the fires
Of mad, bright Summer, ending, sink and pale,
And the last songster from the grove retires
With ling'ring note, that on the air expires.

Brown Autumn gathers in her ripened stores,
The red sun burns through Indian Summer haze,
The ripe nuts patter on the yellow leaves,
The crimson maple sets the hill ablaze;
The red deer, startled from his cool retreat
Down the long forest aisles allures the hound.
With thirsty zeal, hot breath, and lagging feet,
The huntsman follows woodland sight and sound,
Till gathering darkness ends the fruitless round.

These all are vanished, green and fair the fields,
High stands the mansion where the cottage rose:
To smoother hands the yellow harvest yields—
Not truer lives, nor warmer hearts than those
Whom I had known in boyhood's long ago:—
Not braver sons the coming years shall greet,
Nor fairer maidens future lovers know,
Than they who sleep to-day, but rose to meet
The dewy morning with unsandall'd feet.

I cannot know my forest home again,
I cannot be nor feel again a boy,
I cannot taste one hour of vanished pain,
Which now were something near akin to joy.
I cannot meet the sleepers who had toiled
From waking East to slowly dark'ning West—
Whom doubt nor fear in life's rough battle foiled,

To us a heritage, a memory bless'd,
Brave sires and mothers passed unto their rest !

Are they not with us, move around us still ?
In God's half-acre though they lowly lie,
By little church, by brook, or wood, or hill,
This much is left us, all that cannot die,—
Their long, brave struggle, their unfailing hope ;
Their patient trust, their faith in God and man ;
Their patriot zeal, with every foe to cope ;
Nor count their lives a feature in the plan,
But dare for country all that mortal can.

We hold the heritage for which they fought ;
We reap the harvest their strong hands had sown ;
We spend the wealth their lives and labor brought ;
Ours all the fruitage, theirs the toil alone !
Now their mute lips and folded hands impose
On us, their sons, the sacred trust to save
From rude invader's tread, or hand of foes,
The garnished sepulchre, or lowly grave,
Where rest the ashes of the good and brave !

Loud the bugle o'er the valley
Sends its quivering notes afar ;
Rings the answer, rally, rally !
Comes in whispers, Is it war ?

Only cowards need dissemble,
Bravest hearts may danger shun,
Sire with ashy lips may tremble,
When he arms his stripling son !

Yes, 'tis war! across the border,
Proud they come from every state,
Man, and horse, and gun in order,
Nothing left to Heaven or Fate!

Yes, 'tis war! the sad undoing,
All the promise of the years;
But not we by craven wooing,
Shall avert the blood or tears.

Let it come, we wait, are ready!
Sisters pale and mothers weep,
Sweethearts, too.   Hold, boys! Hold steady!
You have hearts and homes to keep.

With you rests your fathers' honor,
They were manly, strong and brave,
Death might find them, later, sooner,
But it could not find a slave.

By you stands your grand old mother,
Firm and faithful, calm and true,
Prestige, power and wealth together,
Past and future pledged for you.

British pluck, and, by that token,
Rose and Shamrock, Thistle dear,
And the "Thin red line" unbroken!
What has Canada to fear?

O'er her homes, by lake and river,
Western plain and Eastern sea,
Waves the Maple Leaf and Beaver,
Union Jack and *Fleur-de-lis!*

Gather, gather, **gather, gather** !
From city mart and sylvan vale,
Side by **side** come son and father,
No one falter, no **one** fail !

Gather gather, **gather,** gather !
From mountain **slope** and ocean blue,
Wife and maiden fair would rather,
If they mourn you, know you true.

Gather, gather, gather, gather !
Fair-haired son from swarthy sire,
Dark-eyed boy from blue-eyed mother,
Saxon brain and Celtic fire.

Cousin is it war ? In story
You would write that you had won,—
We had little left but glory,
Scarce a country, sire or son.—

You have vanquished, **be it** granted,
Seized and **taken at** your will,
All you wished **and** all **you** wanted,
There is something **left us still.**

See ! the battle tide receding—
Is it **victory** ? Cousin, **say,**
Our last **soldier, dying, bleeding,**
Stands above **his flag at bay.**

Prone he sinks in deathly **pallor,**
First and last to duty true ;
Relic of old British valor,—
Still in us, and **still in you.**

Boast your freedom! They who perish
'Neath her banner sow the seed,
Cousin, we together cherish
Freedom born on Runnymede.

Down the silent tide of ages,
Dimly shines her torch afar;
Epochs long, historic stages,
Mould and make us what we are.

Let her dwell in hall or hovel,
Mother shall not nourish slave,
Father shall not cringe nor grovel,
With his birthright, Hampden's grave!

Sceptres may to earth be smitten,
Crowns be old barbaric things;
Long before your code was written,
Cromwell taught the worth of kings.

Bunker Hill to you means glory,
Ours are shrines of heroes too;
Queenston Heights shall live in story,—
Our Canadian Waterloo!

Cousin, Cousin, let us meet you,
Kinsmen by our mighty dead;
By Mount Vernon's shrine we greet you,
Silent, with uncovered head.

Fish and seal? we care but little,
Gulfs, or isles, or open seas;
Ties of blood and kin are brittle,
If they must give way to these!

What matters how the lines be chosen,
Back and forth our children go ;
Welcome **we** our stranger cousin,
Welcome warm as you bestow.

Brothers leave us, fathers follo**w**,
All our bravest, strongest, best,
Seeking homes and harvests yellow,
Somewhere in your golden west !

Maidens fair, **sweet love** compelling,
More than Empire's western star,
Leave Canadian **hall** and sheeling
For some freeborn Lochinvar.

O'er the **border, spite of tariff,**
What has duty **here to do do ?**
What does reckless maiden **care, if**
Smuggled in love's white canoe ?

Wildly o'er the silent valley,
Comes the bugle's note afar,
Loud the echoes, rally ! rally !
Cousin, Cousin ! **is it war !**

Oh might I stay to **see and know, fair land,**
When thou art passing through thy **trying day,**
That wise, and true, **and brave, thy** sons may stand,
To guide **thee safely on thy** higher way ;—

That craven weakling, **caught** in Mammon's toils,
For mess of pottage, or for power or place,
Had not his birthright barter'd for **the** spoils,
Which shall not bless, nor infamy efface,
Of traitor to his country, name and **race.**

I may not stay, the **sun** hath left the sky,
The golden rim hath vanish'd from the **cloud,**
And damp and cold the evening winds go **by,**
And dark o'er all night hangs her solemn **shroud;**
The trees have lost their garniture of green,
The brooklet sleepeth with a silent tongue,
And brown and bare the closing autumn **scene,**
And winter cometh, it shall not be **long:**
And here 'tis fitting I should end my song.

Dear Canada, my home! my song is sung,
A poor, weak tribute which I leave with thee;
I dreamt of nobler things **when life was** young,
But now 'tis all, but if the time should be
When nobler bard may touch a higher strain,
Or wiser seer have brighter tale to tell,
When thou hast travailed through thy birth of pain,
If thou o'er this in retrospection dwell,
'Tis all I ask, Dear Land, Farewell! Farewell!

THE TRAMP.

On a stone by the wayside, half naked and cold,
And sour'd in the struggle of life,
With his parchment envelope grown wrinkled and old,
Sat the Tramp, with his crust and his knife.
And the leaves of the forest fell round him in showers,—
And the sharp, stinging flurries of snow,
That had warned off the robins to sunnier bowers,
Admonished him too, he should go.

But Autumn had gone, having gathered his sheaves,
And the glories of summer were past;
And spring, with the swallows that built in the eaves,
Had left him the weakest and last!
So he sat there alone, for the world could not heal
A disease without pain, without care,—
Without joy, without hope, too insensate to feel,—
Too utterly lost for despair!

But he thought, while the night, and the darkness, and
   gloom,
That gathered around him so fast,
Hid the moon and the stars in their cloud-shrouded
   tomb,
Of the fair, but the far-distant past!
Around him a vision of beauty arose,
Unpainted, unpencill'd by art,—
His home, father, mother, sweet peace and repose,
From the sad *repertoire* of the heart!

And brightly the visions came gliding along,
Through the **warm** golden gates of **the day,—**
With voices of childhood, and music and **song,**
Like echoes from lands far away.
And the glad ringing laughter of girlhood was there,
And one 'mong the others so dear
That o'er his life's record, too black for despair,
Flowed the sad sacred joy of a tear !

And he held, while he listened, his crust, half consumed,
In his cold, shrivelled hand, growing weak,
While a glory shone round him that warmed and illumed
The few frozen tears on his cheek.
In the dark, silent night, thus his spirit had flown,
Like the sigh of a low, passing breath ;—
Life's bubble had burst, and another gone **down**
In the deep, shoreless ocean of death !

In the bright waking morn, by the side of the way,
On the crisp, frozen leaves shed around,
The knife, and the crust, and the casket of clay,
Which the tramp left behind him, were found !
And bound round his neck, as he lay there alone,
Was the image, both youthful and fair,
Of a sweet, laughing girl, with a blue ribbon zone,
And a single white rose in her hair.

Was he loved ? Was she wed ? Was she daughter or wife,
Or sister ?   The world may not read
Her story or his.   They are lost with the life —
Recorded, " A tramp was found dead!"

" Found dead by the way," in the gloom and the cold—
The boy whom a mother had kiss'd,
The son whom a father could proudly enfold,
The brother a sister had miss'd !

" Found dead by the way !" whom a maiden's first love
Had hallow'd—e'en worshipped in part,
And clothed in a light from the glory above,
To enshrine in her pure virgin heart !
Found dead, and alone, by the way where he died,
To be thrown, like a dog, in his lair !
Yet he peacefully sleeps, as the stone by his side,
And rich as the proud millionaire !

TO MARY.

MARY ! the fields are green again,
And flowers are blooming by the river.
Life and beauty gild the plain,
Young and gay and bright as ever.
Spring comes with all its wonted joys,
All its varied rich creation,—
Its shady groves for girls and boys,
Glad with song and animation.

Its ling'ring sunsets, lengthening eve,
Out beyond its winter measure ;
Its dewy morns that rise to leave,
On every blade their pearly treasure.

Things are as always **they have** been,
Side by side in beauty ranging,
Fragrant woods and valleys green;
Mary, only we are changing!

'Tis only we are not the same,
Only ours the tarnished treasures.
Time, that steals **our** youth must claim,
All its dearest, sweetest treasures!
Must dim the pictures one **by** one,
That hope or fancy held before us.
And witness the enchantment gone,
That love or youth exerted o'er us.

The dreams that to fruition rose,
Were not so bright as fancy yielded;
The years that promised us repose,
Brought little rest, when time revealed it.
For though the groves are still **as** green,
And though the birds as glad are singing;
Though vales as verdant lie between
The hills where flowerets still are springing:

Yet Mary, where has every joy,
And wish, and hope, and pleasure vanished,?
Must age life's every charm destroy?
With youth must every dream be banished!
Why should they vanish, all be o'er—
Our evening walks and moonlight roving?
Our idle themes, our sylvan love,
And all our idle dreams of loving?

Why ? Springs that shone for us are fled ;
The flowers they brought are also withered,
And those to-day that deck the mead,
Must be for others grown and gather'd.
The hopes that made us glad are gone,
Like evening shades with darkness blended ;
The birds that sung for us have flown,
The strains we listened to are ended.

The haunts where we in childhood roved,
And fondly longed that youth were over,
And looked and linger'd, laughed and loved,
Have lost their charm to us forever.
For when our dearest friends are dead ;
When those who still remain are colder,
When joys that knit our hearts have fled,
And we as well as they are older :

Then Mary why should we remain,
Or cast a ling'ring look behind us,
On scenes that smile on us in vain,
And but of vanished joys remind us !
Since Mary we have had our day,
Why should we envious gaze on others,
Whose youth, like ours, must pass away,
Whose rest, like ours, is with their fathers ?

Since life at best is but a dream
Which finds youth's heritage expended,
And leaves us little to redeem
The treasure lost, when all is ended :

Then wherefore **sigh we, little** maid ?
The **world** will move along without us ;
So pass we outward **to** the shade,
And wrap our evening cloak about **us.**

—   ..

CASTING FLOWERETS ON THE STREAM.

CASTING flowerets on the stream,
   In the Maytime's merry weather,
Fred and Phyllis, in **a** dream,
   Tied a bud and spray together.

They were children, both, **at** play,
   Startled, as the silent river
Bore the little bud and spray
   Onward from their sight forever.

Phyllis sighed to see them go,
   " Gone ! " she said, and tears had started ;
" Will they on together flow ?
   " Will the bud and **spray** be parted ? "

" **Yes** or no ? " said Fred, and smiled,
   Lightly in a sage endeavor
To console the weeping child,
   Gazing sadly down **the** river.

Answers she by **falling tears,**
   And by silent lips that **tremble;**
Telling **tales** the coming years
   Will have taught **her** to dissemble.

" Back," said **Fred, " we to the** hill,
   Where are other flowers in waiting;
We may pluck them **at** our will,
   Bud and **spray together mating."**

Phyllis, dreamy little **maid,**
   While their hands were locked together,
Look'd from dewy eyes and said,
   "Fred, I do not wish another.

" To-day whatever songs we sing;
   With whatever flowers we deck us;
Back the coming day will bring
   But the faded leaves and echoes !

" I cast the little bud away,
   Heeding naught **if** it should **leave me ;**
It **can never** more be May—
   Fred, it **was** the first you **gave** me !

" Life's deep tide has **not** the **power**
   Back a single joy to give us ;
We have pluck'd **our spray** and flower,
   All but mem'ry's dream must leave us ! "

THE OLD SUGAR CAMP.

THE old sugar camp.
                    There is but little in the name ;
It almost harshly falls upon the ear,
And yields so much the hopeless note of toil,
The strife and struggle of the weary years,
That wealth and plenty from their vantage-ground
Of brighter days, and calm luxurious ease,
May gaze in wonder at the simple shrine,
Where poor devotion pays the vows of age.
And yet, around it cling such memories
As in their acting mould the lives of men,
And give a color to their after-thoughts,
Tinged with the hazy radiance of that past
To which each dusty wayworn pilgrim turns,
When he is sated chasing life's mirage,
And, disenchanted, turns him to the east,
To trace the threads in memory's tangled skein,
Along the strangely checker'd path which time
Has led his footsteps towards—life's western goal.

Here, facing round again, upon youth's morn,
He counts the stages where the nights were spent ;—
Where Hope sat pining, waiting for the dawn ;
But learned, through cycles of the changing years,
That youth had dipped his pictures in the sun
Where time retains the drab,—but dims the gold.
Yet seeks he here some centre for his thoughts,
That wander backward, held at every stage
By some poor fragment in life's broken glass,

Which, lifting sadly **up to memory's** gaze,
He finds a lense that fixes to one spot,
More of the past in stereoscopic guise,
Than all the **others** in that broken whole.

  Thus gathers round a few decaying logs,
That once sustained a rudely-fitting roof,
The same sad longing o'er the vanished **past**
That lifts the hands up to the yews **and** elms,
Where age sits thinking, but where childhood play'd.
For man still, ever shrinking from **the** gloom,
And clouds, and darkness, **round the setting sun,**
Turns to the latest golden glimmer thrown
Back from the turrets **of** his air-built fanes,
Which, in the happy years of long ago,
In that fair Eden whence we all have come,
Rose 'neath the magic wand of youth **and hope.**
Alas! Time's noiseless finger, changing **all,**
Weaves round those shrines the drapery of decay,
Till whereso'er an altar we have raised,
We turn in silence from the crumbling stones,
And learn where'er a human foot has trod, .
We never find the place again the same.

  In that old camp, 'tis many years,
And checker'd years, since the last embers died
Of the last fire that ever shall be lit
By hands now mould'ring in the dust of death.
Back o'er the intervening gulf of time,
I stand once more where, forty years ago,
Dry rustling leaves conceal'd the virgin soil,

And artless wild flowers raised their modest heads,
To taste the sweetness of approaching spring.
These are no more ; a verdant web of grass
Extends thick-matted where the flowers had been.
The underwood is gone, and forest trees
Encumbering the soil are long since burned.
All but a few 'twere sacrilege to touch :
They were the shelter from the rude North Wind
Of those who, safe from all earth's bitter blasts,
Rest in the silent city of the dead.

  Around this lonely pile of wasting logs,
In the strange stillness of the Autumn night,
A few old maples here and there keep watch,
Like silent sentinels that guard a tomb ;
Their fellows fallen many years ago,
Sank from the wounds that ended in decay,
And left them helpless in the northern blast.
Of those now left, kind nature's healing hand
Has cover'd o'er the scars the axe had made ;
But still, as from the poison'd taint of sin,
Their hearts are rotten, and some ruthless gust
Must shortly lay them with their brothers low.
A single butternut, where many stood,
Still stands unnotic'd by the passer-by.
It had its days of interest and pride,
For children watch'd it through the summer months,
As older children watch for autumn stores
In fields and orchards, which that day were not.
'Mid these surroundings other forms arise,
Cold in the moonlight, flitting to and fro,

And shadowy bands, no longer all of earth,
Pass and repass among the spectral trees,
As in the busy scenes of long ago.
The waking Spring returns with sunny morn:
The sap goes coursing through the maple trees,
And ready even with her willing hands
To swell the scanty revenue of toil,
A careful mother, with her happy band,
Goes forth to gather up the liquid stores.
Year after year the old camp fires are lit,—
Year after year the same unbroken band
Prepare the liquid treasure to secure:
And when, upon the first exciting morn,
The axe awoke the echoes of the wood,
The red deer, startled, stood awhile to gaze
On the intruder, and the curling smoke;
Then hasten'd to a covert more secure.

And now began a round of busy weeks.
The nightly frosts, south winds, and vernal sun
Brought forth the forest nectar from the trees,
To lighten labor with a promised gain.
But oft there came a day of sleety snow,
When frost, succeeding, sealed the dripping founts,
And the bleak grimness of a raw March day
Gave to the toilers a much needed rest.
Soon follow'd clearing out of icy pails
And frozen troughs, to wait a brighter time
That only served the labors to renew.

These were the days of anxious toil and care,
When fashions changed not, and the same old coat

Came forth to honor many a gala day ;
And one stern bonnet, brown with sun and rain,
And years of service, still was counted new,
And safely guarded under lock and key
Till Sabbath morn, when forth at duty's call
The faithful wearer trudged o'er many a mile,
To join the songs that are in Zion sung,
And gather up the promises of rest
That faith had treasured in a better clime.

All this the passing years brought to an end.
The days of man and womanhood at length
O'ertook the toilers ; and, with new-born hopes,
New scenes were sought for, and new homes were found.
Caught in the world's wild busy feverish strife,
Beneath one roof-tree now they seldom met.
All but the youngest of the band had gone—
She still remained to grace the dear old home,
And through the calm of uneventful years,
Peace and content appear'd the destined lot.

The calls of want were now no longer known ;
For honest toil had to fruition turned,
And brought its simple harvest of repose.
Yet, as the seasons, in their stately round,
Brought back the flowing to the maple trees,
The old camp-fires rekindled once again—
Glowed with a milder and more chasten'd light.
The old keen busy bustle all was gone,
The feverish care to make the most of time ;
The noisy glee of happy girls and boys
That toy'd with youth, and health, and laugh'd at toil.

All these were o'er.   Yet with each waking year,
As caged swallows, feeling Autumn nigh,
Their wings beat wildly 'gainst their prison bars,
And struggle with their fellows to be free;
So a strange longing to that household came,
To catch the spirit of the vanish'd years,
And catch the woodnotes of the dawning Spring
From songsters turning from their distant climes.
This, and a pride upon the festal board,
To place the treasure gather'd by her hand,
Brought forth the mother and the daughter, still
Beneath the shelter of her childhood's home,
That once again, when happy Christmas time
Brought all together to that dear old home,
And children's children sat upon her knee,
She might bring forth the harvest of her toil.

Thus, the old camp for ten successive springs
Became the miniature of former scenes,
Where just a little for that little's sake,
And for the sake of happy vanish'd hours,
And for the sake of Christmas yet to be,
Was gather'd in a thoughtful, thankful mood,
'Mid chasten'd mem'ries of departed years.
But dark with sorrow rose the gathering gloom
That soon must o'er this calm contentment fall
With poison'd breath, the scourge of Western homes,
Dread dire Consumption, with its certain close,
Had found a victim.   Of that happy pair,
The youngest soon had found a lasting rest.
A single year of painful hope and fear,

And hectic cheek, and bright enkindled eye,
Had left the fatal work of Death complete.
And in that month, and just on such a day
As both had often in the past repair'd
To the old camp, where half in work and **play,**
Their yearly happy holiday was spent,
Brothers and sisters to the loved old home,
Loved for the sake of one no longer there,
Had gather'd for that duty, saddest, last,
To bear a sister to her narrow bed.   .

Sad and bereft, an aged mother stood,
Worn with the struggle of her three-score years,
The light and joy all vanished from her life,
And all the zeal in time's hard battle o'er.
The hands fell down that long were used to toil ;
The mind, elastic still at sixty years,
Turned from the present wholly to the **past,**
Amid the images beyond recall,
To live in mem'ry life's wild dream again,
One more decade still **bound** her to the earth—
Not of it, though remaining **in the** world—
To fill the destined measure of her **days,**
And ripen for **the harvest of the tomb.**

Oh ! what **to her, to us, to any** soul
In that great crisis **which has no** escape,
Is all the wealth **of** gold, **of fame, of** power,
Which life's long struggle gathers **to our** feet ?
When, standing **out on** time's extremest verge,
We gaze **across** the stream with longing eyes,

To catch one gleam of light break through the veil
That hides that ocean whose cold silent wave
No wreckage ever cast on shore of time?
Here she must stand and wait ten weary years,
Her thoughts alone the bread on which she fed;
Her zest in earth's enjoyments, hopes and cares,
Forever vanish'd from her stricken heart,
That longed to reach the haven of its rest,
And hunger'd for a city that abides.
But time, that gathers in our Autumn stores,
And gathers in the fruitage of our lives,
Brought her at last the end that comes to all.
The worn-out heart stood still, to beat no more;
The hands were folded o'er the silent breast;
The eyes forever closed on things of time,
And all earth's glory vanish'd like a breath.

Out from our sight we bear our best belov'd;
We may not linger by their house of clay;
The bier fast follows on the fleeting breath.
She whom we loved was ready for the tomb.
Around stood pioneers with hardened hands,
And eyes but little used to shedding tears;
Yet here with barèd heads they stood and wept,
For she who slept that silent, dreamless sleep
Could not be number'd with the common herd;
And they had loved her in that checker'd past
Which now the haze of time must soon obscure.
So reverently they bore her to her rest,
And turned in silence, leaving her to sleep.

What is there more to tell ? The story ends.
The old camp fires have slept for twenty years,
And, like their builders, never shall awake
The curtain falls o'er one more lowly life,
And there is left but memory of the deeds
Of love and worth that filled three score and ten
Of busy years, along the humble walks
Where only hope was left to sweeten toil,
And only faith was left by buried hope,
To light the pilgrim to the rest of God.

NOT A POET.

Not a Poet ? no, he sings not ;
　　Are not poets sometimes mute ?
Is he greater, he whose bosom
　　Feels the thrill or plays the lute ?

Is the blare of brazen trumpet,
　　Sounded in the ear of Art,
Strong as silver chord that vibrates
　　Through the chambers of the heart ?

Is the voice of Alpine thunder,
　　Calling from its cloud retreat,
Stronger than the brook that murmurs
　　All its music at our feet ?

Is the sigh from wave of ocean,
　　Beating 'gainst life's hither shore,
Stronger as it sinks to silence,
　　Or amid the tempest's roar ?

Thrills not all life's solemn music
 Through the soul's strange woof and warp;
From the monotones of Nature
 On her great Æolian harp?

And the Poet, he who gathers
 All the sad and solemn strain;
Though the why and whence of being,
 Still but *why* and *whence* remain;

Stands he by the Caves of Silence,
 Where the night-winds come and go;
Asking still that awful question,
 Answering winds, " We do not know."

Waits he still, in time-bound fetters,
 Gazing through his prison bars;
Calling out in helpless pleading
 To the cold and voiceless stars.

Thus adown the cycling ages,
 Kneels he at some heathen throne,
Hands upraised to Baal or Moloch,
 Reaching to the Great Unknown.

But the awful *if* that meets him,
 Drifting hopeless from the shore;
Into utter, outer darkness,
 If 'tis darkness, evermore!

But do not the wings of morning
 Wait upon the darkest night?
Is there not a sun still shining
 Always on the shores of light?

Judge him kindly, **if he wanders**
    From the line so plain to thee.
What to some is truth unquestioned,
    He may strangely fail to see.

You may stand where **others** left you,
    He has on and onward trod,
Till no chart will show his **bearing—**
    Is he farther, then, **from God ?**

— — — — —

EVOLUTION ;

OR, THE NEW PHILOSOPHY OF THE UNCON**DITIONED.**

'**TWAS long** before **our** sires were **born**,
While we their babes were sleeping ;
While this old world was young and warm,
She tried her first house-keeping.

And Nature—but the time and place,
Are matter of opinion—
Sat watching somewhere **out in** space,
Where Chaos held dominion.

She saw the steaming waves **go by**,
In angry, fretful brewing,
And thought she'd like some **fish to** fry,
Or set some chicken stewing.

But then the primal egg **was not,**
Nor fish nor fowl to hatch it;
Besides, there was not then a pot,
Nor hook nor line to catch it.

So brooding o'er a little bay,
Where some sea slime had gathered,
She waited, as we wait to-day,
For creatures **foul or feathered.**

With patient zeal **she kept her place,**
Through many a **spring and summer,**
To greet, as **herald of the race,**
The very first new comer.

So looking down 'twixt hope and **doubt,**
In fear the hatch was **lagging,**
She saw two little eyes peep **out,**
A little tail a-wagging!

It was an ancient polliwog,
Had drawn himself together,
And got his molecules agog,
From out the slime his mother.

At first old Nature felt a thrill,
To see the creature wriggle,
And let her happy thoughts **distil,**
In soft maternal giggle.

But when she turned the thing around,
She did not feel contented;
The more she looked, **the** more she found,
It was not what she wanted.

Then o'er her face sped **frown and** pout,—
With two electric flashes,
She turned the creature inside out,
As boarders turn their hashes.

She cast it on an ebbing wave,
Out o'er an angry ocean;
Thus to life's primal germs she gave
The poetry of motion.

But when at length **she dried** her tears,
She thought perhaps that may **be**
She'd spent too many thousand years
In hatching such a baby !

But soon she ceased her angry **pout,**
And furnished the Acarus.*
And showed the biggest thing yet out,
The megaleosaurus !

Then o'er the ancient brine was seen
Some very fishy creatures,
And scaly too, of doubtful mien,
But very open features.

Some protoplasm lay asleep,
And some rough-hewn carmudgeons,
And from the seething, souring heap,
Came forth a pair of gudgeons.

---

*In a work, **Vestiges of Creation**, supposed to have been written by
Robert Chambers, some fifty years ago, the theory of spontaneous gen-
eration was said to be broved by certain experiments carried on by a
Mr. Crosse and afterwards by a Mr. Weeks, from whose researches a
creature called the *Acarus* was evolved from **certain** chemical mixtures
described in the work.

And other forms came rank and rife,
Nautilic and medusic;
Each took a harpy for a wife,
And thus gave birth to music!

At first the brain was but a blob,
Connections, ganglionic;
And from the worst and hardest knob,
Came forth the great Teutonic.

Then swiftly swimming in the van,
Per record sans errata,—
Came something very much like man,—
Lamellabranchiata.

Then round its shining groove elate,
The glad old world went ringing;
One little Indian on a gate,
His boomerang a-swinging.

The stars were singing, all on hand,
The morning rooks were cawing;
And perch'd upon his airy stand,
This "Birdofredum sawin."

In business all began free trade,
Not yet the dream, Protection:
The little Indian's choice was *maid*,
By natural selection.

They met but utter'd not a word,
The manner of their wooing,
Was like the flutter of a bird,—
A mute, internal cooing.

But **yet they** were a happy pair,
Though language still was lacking,
There burst upon the startled air,
A loud primeval smacking.

But words at length began to come,
At first from kiss came kissing;
For love was often found from home,
As now, he went a *missing!*

They **took** the stage in dishabille,
A custom **still** prevailing;
They faced the devil in their peel,
Nor found their courage failing.

First act in bower of garden fair,—
Thus **runs** the tale in chapel,
But **soon** the wisest, sweetest pair,
Had **ate the sourest apple.**

Then seemed their morning wardrobe scant,
Their *robe de nuit* felt thinner;
They could no longer play at cant,
So tried the role of sinner.

Their children wander'd East and West,
So runs the fact or fable;
Some stayed at home and tried their best
To build the tower of **Babel.**

But strive or struggle as they would,
The end was always sorrow;
'Twas sometimes famine, sometimes flood,
But last, and **worst,** Gommorah!

So now the races are but three,
The Saxon, Celt, and Cuffy ;
When Nature fixed his family tree,
She was a little huffy.

The Hindu, Chinaman, and Jap,
They may be taken solid ;
And then per million or per cap,
They may be labelled stolid.

Just wise enough for little trade,
For little truck and barter ;
But not the stuff from which is made
A rebel or a martyr.

The Irishman is hard to place ;
This much is safely written,
That Britain means to him disgrace,
And he disgrace to Britain !

The Saxon, too, is all awry,
The Celt, 'tis hard to teach him ;
Poor Cuffy was hung out to dry,
Before 'twas tried to bleach him.

Though Nature knew the venture made,
Her old repute might tarnish,
She forced poor Sambo on the trade,
In paint, but little varnish.

So thus he stands half-done to-day,
All head and gab and gullet ;
Emerging from the far away,
An evoluted mullet,

Made up of many a human note,
With light and shade insertion ;
He waits at Jordan for a boat,
He does not like immersion.

To get the Celt upon the stage,
There were some jars and hitches ;
He up and started in a rage,
To rough it, sans his breeches.

But he was born to push his way,
'Gainst Saxon, Thug, or Spartan ;
So stands before the world to-day
In sporran, dirk and tartan.

He has his politics, 'tis true ;
But though of Grits the grittest,
His faith is bounded by the view,—
" Survival of the fittest ! "

ANOTHER **OLD** APPLE TREE.

" This fruit forbidden, children hence ! "
Said surly canine, tall rail fence ;
Both now removed from present tense,
　　As all life's glories are !
It stood against the morning sky,
With gnarled trunk, and branches high ;
Some green, some withered, old and dry.
　　With promise faint and far.

It bore but small and scraggy fruit,
And high it hung: 'twas green to boot—
One end was oblate, one acute,
    And hard as hard could be.
But Ame **and I,** we always found,
If north or south on duty bound,
The shortest, straightest way was round
    By that old apple tree !

We sought its shade one luckless day,
When flowers, found blooming by the way,
Were leagued with folly, whisper'd **"stay,"**
    Though wisdom said " abstain."
We struggled hard, **we struggled long,**—
Weighed first the danger, last the wrong ;
But pleasure sung her sweetest song,
    " Who heedeth future pain ? "

We stood with longing in our look,
Till down went dinner, basket, book,
And then the limbs we gently shook,
    With circumspection meet.
Down came the bait, and if we stole,
We reasoned, " Surely on the whole,
The guilt was with the wicked pole,
    That brought it to our feet !"

Alas ! the farmer saw the loot,
And broke the charm with howl and hoot ;
I faced the dog,—Ame seized the fruit.
    We longed to be at school !

More welcome learning's **thorny** way,
Than terrors of this judgment **day,**—
More lurid, in a striking way,
        Than master's rod or rule!

First round, the canine fell on top;
My calves were sore, I wished he'd stop;
And Amy, too, was like to drop,
        From fear and dog allied.
Success may pain and conscience drown,
But what availed for me renown,
When stitch that held my **braces down,**
        Was found **in** Amy's **side.**

The struggle ended dishabille,
I, pain and shame from head to **heel,**
All one big nerve, its function, *feel,*
        And life **a solemn thing.**
I stood like Indian warrior dressed,
One nether limb, abraised, distressed,
Hung through the armhole of my vest—
        My pants were in the ring.

Our dinners? Well, in short, **were not,**
Our hearts were sore, our faces hot,
Our reputation gone to pot—
        That apple must atone
For net results, our wounded pride,
Our buns and eggs in butter fried,
All safe and warm the dog's inside—
        That apple left alone,

Soon bite alternate stained **our** lips
Of green outside and snowy pips,
Till fingers brown with acid drips,
    Had fed us **core** and stem.
Let Mercy weep in Eden's bower,
If dwellers there knew more the power
Of evil, in temptation's hour,
    Than we, then pray for them.

Ame's shoes, I know, were holes and rips ;
Dark crescents graced her finger tips,
But Love's sweet bow hung o'er her lips,
    And O ! her eyes were brown.
I know to-day the fruit was sour,
But O ! 'twas Summer's morning hour—
And you may too have felt the power
    Of eyelids drooping down.

And you were there, and life was young,
Nor erred in thought, in deed, or tongue ;
In stately pride and virtue strong,
    O braver heart than mine !
But some have prayed while you have slept,
O'er sins unspoken, vows unkept,—
O'er soul in travail, wailed and wept ;
    Some nobler hearts than thine !

Go, change thy level head for gold,
Thy hollow heart for mines and mould ;
Then bring it, pulseless, slimy, cold,
    A gift to Mammon's shrine !

Who cares thy brother goes unfed ?
In shame thy sister hangs her head ?
If thou art clothed, and warmed, and fed,
  With purple, oil, and wine !

The years depart, their ghosts abide,
Like shadows dancing on the tide,
Which waves soon carry far and wide,
  As leaves of that old tree !
O, Amy, child, do you still know,
This bitter sweet of long ago ?
Or lies the little maiden low,
  That brings those dreams to me ?

PARTED.

ALL night a wave had travelled o'er the main,
And in the morning kiss'd the sunlit shore ;
The broken waters backward roll'd again,
To meet or mingle in that wave no more.

Through all the cycling ages yet to be,
The sever'd atoms o'er the waters ride ;
Nor shall they gather e'en on unborn sea,
'Neath newlit sun, to mingle with its tide.

Nor shall they meet again in morning dew,
Nor mists that build the palaces of cloud ;
Nor painted bow, with all its golden hue,
Borne on the bosom of its own dark shroud.

A lily spread its petals to the sun,
Another morn the lily was not there ;
Its pure life's lesson and its labor done,
Its soul far floating on the trembling air!

Its gathered beauty from the earth and sky,
Its warm, sweet perfume, like a maiden's breath,
Had met and mingled, vanish'd like a sigh,
And pass'd forever to the realms of death.

At morn a rose hung deck'd with silver gem,
At noon 'twas wither'd, of its grace bereft :
At eve the fragrance linger'd round the stem,
Another morn, its place alone was left !

O lily fair ! queen of your bright domain,
Where poets dream, and youth and beauty meet ;
How quickly gather'd back to death again !
How rudely scatter'd all that made you sweet !

O bright, sweet rose ! on virgin's bosom worn,
Fair emblem of our life's short joy and pain ;
Thy glory fled, why must thy lingering thorn,
Like love's dead dream and buried hopes remain ?

Of all the vanished nights, must that too, fade ?
So glad with moon and star, and summer air ;
And breath of flowers, and mingling light and shade,
For lovers sent, two lovers who were there.

They sang their hymn of Eden in the grove,
They watched the moonbeams trembling through the
    leaves ;

They dream'd their dream, their sad, sweet dream of
    love ;
They gather'd only mem'ry-laden sheaves.

Two hearts awoke to love's wild pulse of joy,
That yet must learn what pain such hearts can bear ;
When sire must weep above his sleeping boy,
And mother lay to rest a daughter fair.

They stood beside two lonely little graves,
Without a stone, they knew who slept below ;
They cared so little for what marble saves,
But could they only lift the veil and know,—

That in that heaven of pearly gate and street,
Of pure white robes and saintly spirits, there,
They too, should yet behold, and kiss, and meet
Those warm young lips, bright eyes, and golden hair.

They kept this solemn sabbath of the soul,
In silent worship, with their hearts bereft ;
Then turned them sadly towards life's western goal,
With Oh ! so little worth the living left.

They wander'd outward to the shoreless main,
Love's dream, their youth, and summer's glory fled ;
With hearts still lingering o'er the sad refrain,
Of music dying. Hope, the minstrel, dead !

A pilgrim rested by a ruin'd tower,
Weary he waited in the twilight grey ;
All he had loved since youth till this dark hour,
The hungry grave had swallow'd as its prey.

And parted, scatter'd far through every clime,
　Were hearts which dust to dust had handed o'er
To the eternal change of space and time,
　Through all duration's endless evermore!

MY ISLAND HOME.

O sing not to me of your tropical glories,
　Of the land of the orange, the fig or the vine,
Though unclouded the sun may unsparingly pour his
　Warm rays o'er its bosom, still dearer is mine;
Still dearer the land which moss-circled daisy
　And wild mountain heather bedeck with their bloom,
Where the hero still dreams by the brook, winding mazy
　Among the green vales of his own Island Home!

Among the green vales, where careless his childhood,
　Untrammell'd by fashion, delighted to stray,
And twine on the hill, 'neath the shade of its wildwood,
　A wreath to be worn but in life's opening day,
Ere the fast rising waves of life's stormy ocean
　Should leave him no more thus unheeding to roam,
Or the dark daring struggle of war's wild commotion
　Divide him by death from his dear Island Home!

Where love's waking joys early taught him to ponder
　On visions of greatness seen beaming afar,
And hopefully led him, e'en erring, to wander
　And gather a name 'mid the glories of war.

Yet sing not to me of rich **streams from** your mountains,
  Of your valleys of diamonds or pearl-gilded foam,
For dearer to me are the rills from the fountains
  That flow 'mong the hills of my own Island Home!

'Mong the hills of my home, the land of my fathers,
  The birthplace of heroes, untrodden by slave,
Where Liberty gems for its coronet gathers,
  'Mong names of the mighty, from rolls of the brave;
Where the rude minstrel's song in its wild rustic numbers,
  Though to pale pedant lore and to science unknown,
Awakes in each bosom the soldier that slumbers—
  The glory to guard of his dear Island Home!

Of the land where the ashes **of** patriots sleeping,
  Lie pillarless, left on the fields where they fell,
Yet safe rest the names from Oblivion in keeping,
  That sacred to freedom in memory dwell!
And kindle a warm and undying devotion
  In the breasts of her children wherever they roam,
Till " the green vales of Scotland " means one with emotion
  To each wandering son of that dear Island Home!

Where still from her valleys to melody rising,
  Sounds far up the mountain the bard's melting strain;
Where fearless her children, oppression despising,
  The terror of tyrants unchanging remain.
Then sing not to **me of rich streams from** your fountains,
  Of your valleys of diamonds or pearl-gilded foam,
When dearer to me are the rills from the mountains
  That flow through the vales of my own Island Home.

MOODS OF BURNS.

(Toronto Caledonian Society's Silver Medal Prize Poem. Awarded
Jan., 1885.)

WELCOME frae Strath, and glen, an' toun,
Frae far an' near, frae hut an' ha';
I'm unco' fain as time brings roun'
This nicht again, to meet ye a',
Assembled here at mem'ry's ca',
To bring the by-gane days to min',
And gather frae the far awa'
The sad, sweet notes o' Auld lang Syne.

Ye've come in honor o' our bard,
The pleughman o' the banks o' Ayr,
Wha sang love's joys and worth's reward,
Amid his heritage o' care ;
'Mid a' the dool he had to bear,
His heart still warmed at nature's ca';
Wee cowrin mouse an' wounded hare,
He was a brither to us a'.

Wha cares what spot ye ca' your hame,
Frae north to south o'er Scotland fair ;
Ye're loyal brither Scots the same,
Your passport this, we ask nae mair.
So bid ye welcome a' to share,
In homage to the "soul of song,"
Wha left in trust to Scotland's care,
The fame that must to Time belong.

Ye're maybe frae the source o' Dee,
Frae Bonnie Doon or Annandale,
Frae Ballochmyle or Craigielea,—
Frae Yarrow's holms or Lanark vale ;
Or maybe ye're frae Crief or Crail,
Frae Aberdeen, or there awa';
Still kith or kintra's no the hale,
Ye ken "A man's a man for a'".

Or ablins ye're frae Carrick side,
Frae dank loch Goil or Locher fell,
Frae Frith o' Forth or Strath o' Clyde,
Or frae Gleniffer's dewy dell.
If south the Tweed ye've chanced to dwell,
Or in the isle o' Tara's ha',
Just keep that slily to yoursel ;
Ye'll maybe, be a man for a'.

Ye're maybe frae the heathery hills,
Frae bauld Brae Mar, or Ben Macdhu ;
Sons of the moorlands, rocks an' rills,
A Highland welcome waits for you.
An' gin ye're manly, leal an' true,
Although our Bard has gaen awa',
He's left ye lasses fair to loe,
Nae matter how your lot may fa'.

In his bright roll ye canna want,
Ye've Chloris, Maggie, Jean an' May ;
An' gin your beef or brose be scant,
Ye'll aye at least a haggis hae ;

Then why to gruesome care gie way,
Gin hock or port ye canna prie;
Ye aye can make ae happy day,
While ye hae still the barley bree.

Ye're maybe but a pleughman lad,
That whistles lightly owre the lea;
Then tak' your bonnet an' your plaid,
Your Nannie's at the trystin' tree;
An' she is fair an' young an' free,
An' leal to you through good and ill,
By Lugar's stream she waits for ye,
Man! you're a monarch, come what will!

But maybe ye are auld an' grey,
An' doon the brae ye hirple slow;
But min' ye man ye've had your day!
Come ben John Anderson my Joe,
Your spouse sits at the ingle lowe,
An' she is croose and canty still,
Wi' blessings on your frosty pow;
Haith John, ye hae na fared sae ill!

If death's snell wintry blast's blown owre,
Love's youth its plighted joys to kill,
Your Mary's only gaen before,
Yon ling'ring star's aboon ye still.
An' roun' Montgommery's castle hill,
The flowers o' faith an' hope still bloom,
Life's purest joys Time canna fill,—
'Tis but the dust that seeks the tomb.

Amang the mools Death wraps our cares,
But through that gate we a' maun gae,
The Cotter's hope, the Patriot's prayers,
Remain to cheer us by the way.
But not alone life's gloamin' grey,
For light to gild, we bless our Bard,
But Patriot fire, for manhood's day,
Our foes to meet, our rights to guard !

Then let invasion draw her blade ;
She'll find us strike as well as draw,—
They're nae a' dead, the Light Brigade !
Ha'e up an' at them Forty Twa ;
An' Coldstream Guards up an' **awa'!**—
Charge Enniskillen an' Scots Grey !
An' gather Cameron men an' a',
Ho up ! an' rally Scots wha hae !

Brave Saxon brithren, while ye boast,
O' England's glory, England's gains ;
Oh reed ye ever a' it cost,
In Celtic fire and Doric brains !
When Scotia pays 'mid strife and **pains,**
The victor's death to honor due ;
Then 'mid her tartans' crimson stains,
Gives o'er the dear won prize to you.

Dear Scotia ! frae this western shore,
We look to thee across the sea,
With faith the stronger, love the more,
Because our Bard has sung in thee.

We know the glory yet to be,
Must largely rest with thee an' thine;
An' bless for homes and altars free,
The great and good o' Auld Lang Syne!

EPISTLE TO A PLAGIARIST.

F. WELLESLEY PORTER,—Finn or Frank,
Or Fred, or Theophrastus Such ;
I'm wac to think your silly prank,
Should pu' a bardie doun sae much
I wasna tapmaist i' the class,
I stood a bittie down the raw ;
But didna think ye should hae less,
E'en had they gi'en ye goud an' a'.

I see'd ye had a classic stride,
An' high an' wide ye flapp'd your wings,
I see'd,—I ken na what beside,—
Ay, gore, an' war, an' swords, an' things ;
I see'd much beauty in your sang,
Poetic figures i'st they ca'
The host that dance in fancy's thrang,
An' a' her fairy pictures draw.

I glinted up, but vainly sought
To see your bird the cluds amang ;
I heard its note, but little thought,
'Twad split its weasand wi' its sang !

I see'd your robin on the hearth,
Your lark I never see'd ava,
For when the *foul* was brocht to earth,
My certes, it was but a craw !

Man, if the lass that loes ye best,
An' kens ye're sic a pawky dog,
Wad like a star upo' your crest,
Just hing your medal at your lug.
When she looks up wi' love elate,
An' thinks how much is in a name ;
Admit 'tis charming to be great,
But, oh, the slipp'ry paths o' fame !

If some wee laddie takes your han',
Wha ca's ye daddie, dad, or da,
An' wishes sair to be a man,
An' sees his model in his pa ;
Or some wee lassie, fair and sweet,
Looks up to you in winsome glee,
In whom her mither's smile ye meet,
Her mither's face, her mither's e'e.

Then tak your silver medal doun,
While they admire wi' infant pride,
An' think ye worthy o' a croun
O' laurel wreath, an' bays beside.
Life's flowery byways lie before,
The gilt an' glare bedaze their eyes ;
They feel youth's fire, an' long to soar,
Ye tell them how to win the prize.

Ye teach them **that to win a name,**
How needless 'tis to sweat and moil,—
Ye ken a shorter road to fame,
An' wealth, an' worth, than honest toil.
Ye ken the brazen jade pretence,
An' dawds o' cheek tak longer **strides,**
Than **truth** an' **brains** an' common **sense,**
An' often gain **their** end besides.

Ye **choose** your **motto like the lave,**
Let faith an' truth an' **a'** be lost;
But from the wreck **of** Manhood **save,**
The gaud, " Success **at any** cost !"
Let worth gae **whistle to the win'** ;
Let honor pack her kit **an' sail** ;
Let **shachel-leggit sham come in,**
An' **be successful, that's the hale !**

He **Heigh, Porter, man, ye needna tried**
The **rhyming britherhood tae hurt** ;
They hae that silly **thing ca'd pride,**
That keeps them maistly **oot the dirt.**
I'm fear't **ye dinna read your Burns,**
For there, that man's the man for a',
Wha's **honest** pride indignant spurns,
What touches honor's highest **law.**

I hope ye're but a thowless boy,
Wham some wild youthfu' freak has led
To mingle **wi'** your base alloy,
The gems **ye plunder'd from the** dead.

But noo' your wee bit pride to hain'
I'll say nae mair, but just tak tint,
That after this the bairn's your ain
Afore ye kirsen it in print.

THE AGE OF PROGRESS.

The following extracts are from a poem written some thirty-nine years ago, when Spiritualism, Free Love and Phrenology, were at their best, so far as the lecturers' harvest in these fields was concerned. At that time I have known L. N. Fowler, O. Leroy and others give courses of lectures on Phrenology, Matrimony, and kindred subjects, when it was difficult to secure sitting room at a Dollar a night in the Galt Town Hall, which I think would seat comfortably at least 500 persons. The excitement consequent on these lectures gave rise to the poem, of which only portions are here given.

At that time, also, Slavery was an active living fact in American Life, which accounts for some of the allusions found in the poem.

THIS is the age about which sages write,
Not saintly wholly, nor millennial quite ;
If superstition be to cloisters fled,
Knaves still survive, and folly is not dead.
If progress high and wide her banner waves,
Its shadow falls upon a thousand graves ;
From the cold face of the departed years,
She gathers gems, but finds them frozen tears ;—
Finds thousands toil, and sweat, and weep and wear,
To deck the palace of a millionaire ;
Finds gospel fakirs* plant and spread their tent,
To save poor sinners at so much per cent.,

---

*A pair of religious fakirs spoken of as converted Jews, struck the Town of Galt, about twenty-four years ago, and set all the religious

Divide the spoils with sharpers in the fold,
Who take from ravens either bread or gold ;
Allot one share, perhaps the church to paint ;
While one buys diamonds for luxurious saint,
Or swells his purse to cherish some abuse,
Or purchase silver for his table use.*

Oh yes! 'tis doubt and dread on every hand,
Who scapes on sea encounters sharks on land ;
Cowards with swords, and beggars in black coats,
And all have beards, †we cannot tell the goats ;
Lawn-throated thieves who scape a hempen cord,
But wait the Summer of a Dives' reward.
We cannot, through hypocrisy and cant,
Detect the greatness of a bogus saint ;
The mildly good lack all the genius deep
Of prowling wolves that pose and pass for sheep ;
For who can judge of vice adorned in ruffles,
Tyrants in chains, or beauty hid in muffles,
Some masquers lavish hot, impassioned kisses,
On wither'd hags for sentimental misses ;

---

people of the place by the ears. After a time they were discovered to be thorough scoundrels, who over their hot brandy, laughed at the gullability of their victims ; ran jewelry and other bills, which they never paid ; while one of them, some time afterwards, was reported to be the hero of a notorious case of betrayal and desertion, which took place in one of our Northern Counties.

*The famous Table Silver escapade, which took place a few years ago, and came to light while the principal in the affair was posing as an Evangelist in Toronto, is a case in point.

†Forty years ago it was thought to be very unclerical to wear a full beard or mustache.

Some take **an heiress** with her **gold in barter,**
And spend their future fencing with a **tartar.**
And to be mistress of the grounds and cottage,
Some take the nursing of a churl in dotage.
What of it all ? The money's hers of course,
Romances sometimes finish with divorce,
'Neath whose kind sway Misogynists may **bear**
To take a trip on Matrimony's **car.**
And if they find the journey long or rough,
Take a mild exit at some switching **off;**
And when their troubles have gone **out of mind,**
Renew the pleasure if they feel inclined.

O happy age, when every theme is bright,
And every prospect promises **delight;**
If little sins should terminate **in sorrow,**
The great escape, and need not fear **to-morrow.**
Rejoice all ye who flourish pregnant purses,
Ye hold a passport from the two worlds' curses;
Well pleased with this, to lose **the other loath,**
And wisely grasping all ye **can of** both.
If now and then a straggling **sunbeam** must
Pierce the soul's darkness, and display **the** dust,
What need that conscience grate beneath conviction,
While oil of Mammon **will** destroy **the** friction.
If sinners finishing a drunken **revel,**
Get midnight views of Hades and the devil
And then his regions for prolonged enjoyment,
When earth denies them pity or employment.
'Tis not your crime, *you* but the profits draw,
While *they,* poor yahoos, **have got drunk** by law.

Well, have them gaoled, and jugged; for mercy sake,
Our statutes punish crimes they help to make.
If unwed mothers seek some dark retreat,
Or find no mercy till a winding sheet,
Let their betrayers seek the glorious west,
And sink into redundancy of rest.
Or, turning seers, console their victims with
A late improved edition of Joe Smith.

But 'tis not all a single-handed game,
For ardent chase can yield no conquest tame ;
Take one example, as some poet says,
Of hopeless love, the love of latter days.
Don Pedro dwelt beside the Susquehanna,
Where saints and sages whistle " O, Susanna ! "
His sire, a Portuguese of noble birth,
Loved a Madonna of Italian earth ;
And with her after to Columbia roves,
When Don was born to seal their happy loves ;
Thus he was sprung from two impassioned races,
With hearts as sentimental as their faces ;
But being both a gentleman and scholar,
His tastes craved more and more the mighty dollar.

His heritage but yielded scanty sesters,
To cultivate Monte Carlo or a mistress ;
Yet was he styled a fascinating fellow,
With poverty his hell, his heaven duello.
Like many other men, or maids, or books,
The world knew nothing of him, save his looks.
And these ? Take first a face not Saxon wholly,
And eyes like Spanish maids', half melancholy ;

Dark eyebrows arched, and a nose Circassian,
Teeth almost pearly, whiskers almost Russian.
All this had touched the fair, who never spoke,
So many hearts were wounded, some were broke.
Don, heedless of the mischief he might make,
Moved heedless on, nor loved for mercy's sake ;
Till some assumed he must be sour or cold,
And others fancied he was getting old.
Alas ! that fact unmasks the best disguise,
Don, all the while, was waiting for a prize,
So caught, at last, the fortune-hunter's fever,
Then passed the iceberg from his mood forever.

He left his home, 'twas said for recreation,
But wiser heads believed 'twas speculation.
He sailed from Cincinnati in a ship
That peddled niggers down the Mississip.
The master plied with tale, and joke, and laughter,
Don learned the owner had a lovely daughter,
And that he was a planter, fast and wild,
And she, the daughter, was an only child.
Don's heart, or pocket, felt a strange unquiet,
Such feelings sometimes spring from change of diet.
But out on pleasure, not in haste, however,
He'd see the girl, she dwelt just by the river.
And to his friend the master ? he, if luck shone,
Might count some louis on an introduction,
Which came in course.   Don Pedro met the lady.
The day was warm, but Inez's bower was shady,
And all as fair as lover could express,
By thought or wish to lead him to success.

On love's bright chessboard he knew all the moves,
Of lead or follow, as the fair one proves
Self-willed or docile, prone to watch the hook,
Or yield unwooed, unwon, to smile or look.

Don knew each art that could amuse or please,
And played each part with subtle grace and ease.
He held love's coin, and multiplied its magic,
Used all the arguments in Cupid's logic;
He knew that Inez was a worthy prize,
So used the silent language of his eyes,
Which, added to the sweetness of his tongue,
Seemed fatal ordnance 'gainst a heart so young.
But when that fortress stood by all unshaken,
Don felt impatience in his breast awaken,
So told his amorata the next day,
That on the morrow he must go away ;
Business was pressing, then sans fuss or fustian,
" Inez," said he, " I hope you are a Christian."
This startled Inez, and his friends would, too,
For all believed Don Pedro was a Jew.

But when in love, whatever saints say of it,
The fair may worship Allah or his prophet.
But to our tale.   Don Pedro could not go,
The prize was worthy, but the work was slow.
All subterfuge and idle play must stop,
Straight to the point, " Sweet Inez, may I hope."
Sweet Inez saw what he would be about,
And, half in pity, helped the fellow out,
Yet coolly watching for some nobler game,
Denied, if ever she had felt a flame,

This was the death-blow of Don Pedro's bliss,
" Love's dream is o'er, and brings it only this,"
He said, and laid his hand upon his heart.
" Inez farewell," said, too, with princely art ;
And lastly said, when turning to the river,
" Oh, cruel fair, I'm desolate forever."

And so he seemed, for evening found the Don
Howling his disappointment to the moon
Beside the Mississippi, where he strayed,
Wrapt in dark purpose of a Lethal shade.
But yet 'tis hard to die without a name,
Unloved, forgotten, melancholy, tame,
By hope forsaken, woman e'en unkind.
He poured his sorrows on the waves and wind,
And prayed the stars for pity. So began
Don Pedro's dark soliloquy on man.

" Thou silvery moon, thou mild attendant star,
Whose beams, commingling, travel from afar
To light and cheer this busy scene of man—
This maze of being without end or plan,
For what is man ? What, even in his prime ?
A bubble floating on the sea of time,
Who, in life's morn, 'mid Hope's bright visions sings,
Nor heeds what sorrow from to-morrow springs,
But laughs and weeps with every change he sees,
Like hour-lived insects floating on the breeze.

" Oh, Jupiter, of stern and awful brow,
Before whom all the other godlings bow ;
Whose throne is highest on Olympus' mount,
Ye nymphs that revel at Castalia's fount,

Thou wingèd boy, whose shaft has pierced e'en me,
And thrown poor Sappho headlong in the sea :
Ye endless hosts down to Arcadian Pan,
Who war and weep and dance and sing for man,
Why must he live to discontent and pain,
Why born to act but Death's dark scene again ?
Why cursed with endless longing to be great,
But still the plaything of unbending Fate ?
And last, Why Fortune 'gainst all higher rules
Withholds her favors to bestow on fools ? "

Thus Don continued in misanthrope mood,
Till wrath and railing seemed to do him good,
For soon his back was turned to the water,
And all his passion for the planter's daughter
Was turning too : for Don, alas, was human,
He wanted gold, but could have spared the woman.

Dear languid belles, such are the parasites
That haunt your days and serenade your nights ;
Awake the hopes that vanish ere your youth,
As do your loves, all false and fungus growth,
Which e'en in childhood springs around your heart,
Cankering and eating every nobler part,
Till, like some bow which long has idle hung
In some old hall forgotten, not unstrung,
When found its power to throw the shaft has flown,
Its strength and elasticity are gone ;
And so with you, the tears of maidenhood
O'er paper loves and paper heroes shed,
Take so much tension that your bright ideal
Leaves little warmth of love to spare the real,

And finds your lives tame, commonplace and cold,
When every feeling is by Art made old.

FOGIES.

Friends, foes and citizens, lend me your ears,
I ask you not for sympathy or tears,
If this unchangeable last stroke of Fate
Awakes not love it surely bankrupts hate.
You know this carcass here, that only waits
The deadman's cart to pass it through the gates,
He was your townsman—Deacon in the church,
And taught his sons religion with a birch.
High in his day, and very orthodox,
He knew the martyrs as contained in Fox;
His creed was very short, but very strong,
With reasons more than others, twice as long.
His labor ethics for their author speak
Twelve hours a day and seven days a week.
All other time gave generously away,
As July first, on twenty-fourth of May.
Behold him now, no friend to claim his dust,
Interred by strangers, just as strangers must.

I will not ask, Had he a nobler part?
How much of soul, how much of head or heart?
It profits not I should on virtues dwell,
To you, long doubtful, let me therefore tell
How *he*, for long a figure on your street,
Lies low to-day and cold beneath a sheet.
'Twas thus the final ending came about,
You all remember, some too well, no doubt;

When first the wave of Progress struck our town
And turned our old-time notions upside down,
He could not change nor act a second part,
No power could reach his head or touch his heart.
He raged, he fumed, he fretted and he fried,
They called him "poor old fogie," and he died.
Died 'mid the fierceness, froth and foam that springs
From mad devotion to terrestrial things.
Died thus : for forced aside into the cold,
I found him homeless, friendless, feeble, old.
And dazed and listless, on the busy street ;
And wandering idly with uncertain feet ;
His stock awry, his garments thin and torn,
A stranger in the town where he was born.

Alas ! how changed from him we used to know,
In his bright Heyday of the long ago ;
When steam was young, and progress had not come
To spoil his visions, and to strike him dumb.
Unyielding still, immutable as fate,
Too firm to swerve, too proud to change his gait.
Too slow to learn, too over quick to know,
Too prone to strife, to give or take a blow,
Keen in polemics, and in science sure,
Certain in all things, and in motives pure.

I do remember when our town begun
To learn about the planets and the sun ;
When wandering sages in our halls each night,
Snuffed out our candles with their stellar light ;
Set up the spheres, the milky-way unfurled,
And changed its nebulosity to world.

To him 'twas lunacy of darkest dye,
Nor was there poverty of reason why,
He saw and knew, and felt, the earth was flat,
The sun no bigger than a Quaker's hat;
He knew the sun and stars, how far or near,
Were all to light our egotistic sphere !
What though the moon did sometimes go astray,
And burn her waning rushlight through the day ;
What though she sometimes, too, forgot to light
Her little taper in the darkest night.
To him no barrier rose to strain belief,
What fault of his, if science came to grief.
He put it thus, " My friend you cannot feed,
A lusty offspring on agnostic creed,
Hence I approve and patronize the Devil,
And not a myth personified, as Evil.
I hold a lake of brimstone flaming hot,
Is something better than just 'go to pot !'"

Oh worthy deacon, never in the lurch,
None abler fought the battles of the church ;
Alas ! that now a toot you cannot hear,
From Zion's towers or turrets, far or near.
Death's lusty breakers caught you on the hip,
And left you stranded like a broken ship.

Friends, thus it came about our townsman died,
Not cold, in want, nor comforts unsupplied.
You will recall, I found him faint and thin,
Cold and unclad, deserted by his kin ;
A victim bankrupt in the race of mind,
Left by his fellows many leagues behind.

I wept to think the fogie race was o'er,
That broad fat faces must be seen no more ;
'Twas not harmonious, 'twould incongruous seem,
Among lank shadows of a Pharaoh's dream.
I sorrowed that their honest work was done,
For now the **age of** reason **had** begun.

But **what !** alas ! O must **I** live to see
A **race neglected, so** beloved **by** me ?
Worse **than neglected, driven from the stage,**
And doomed to bear contumely **with age.**
It **shall not** be, for still Arcadian Pan
Is **still** a god, and still **he cares** for man ;
Then see my cot on **yonder mountain glow,**
Above the **rabble of the vale below,**
Where sun and **shade** in pleasing **dalliance play,**
And streamlets **murmur to the closing day** ;
Behold my **vineyard on its shaggy brow,**
And goats **that labor in my wooden plow.**
Behold my wine-press after Noah's model,
Wine to inspire, but **not confuse the noddle.**

Behold my flocks, my **little mountain maid,**
The **guardian angel of the peaceful shade.**
Behold **my wealth, my couch** of fragrant moss,
My home, my all, **my ottoman of grass** ;
My bow unerring, **to procure** you game—
These, with my energies, your virtues claim.
Then come, dear fogies let us dwell together,
What though despised, if dear to one another.
Come lingering relics of a by-gone age,
Come to my cottage—I will be your page.

Pleased will I listen to your midnight song,
Of deeds accomplished when your hearts were young ;
And gaze approving at your rising joys,
As memory wakes the scenes when ye were boys ;
Or fancy paints again your happy lot,
'Mid rustic innocence to-day forgot ;
Till once again ye tread youth's sacred groves,
Bright with the visions of your vanished loves.
Or watch awhile, awakened thought pursue,
Some darker theme to autumn's sombre hue ;
Till, 'mid your dreams, involuntary start
Tears o'er some sad bereavement of the heart.

O come ! dear fogies in a stranger's land,
Among a race ye cannot understand.
Believe me almost sharer in your tears,
And glad to comfort your declining years.
No need to tell how much I feel like you,
My little maid feels all your sorrows too.
Come, we shall watch around your dying bed,
And smooth your pillow, and adjust your head
And as the spirit leaves each honest breast,
Will lay a fogie with his sires at rest ;
Raise o'er his grave a monumental stone,
To be remembered, if by *us* alone !

'Twas thus we cared for, thus a fogie died ;
We closed his eyes, and laid his faults aside ;
Heard all his hopes, and witnessed all his pain,
And knew we would not see his like again !
Oh ! brother, have you ever seen the tears
Which mem'ry wrings from out the shroud of years ?

Or heard the notes that **vibrate o'er the strings,**
When second childhood to first childhood sings ?
They **come so far o'er** vanished time and **space;**
Pass in such flashes o'er the aged face,
You feel the world, where **each** has but **his day,**
Has just **one Spring,** one **single** month of May;
We rule to-day, to-morrow yield our place,—
We all are fogies, to the coming race !

"Come bright improvement **on the car of Time!"**
So sung the bard, and we improve the rhyme,
Enjoy the blessings his **petition** sought,
And more than love or **mercy** would have brought.
Progression's tide has to a **deluge rose,**
And from earth's bosom swept her **dreamy foes.**
Hurled priests and bigots to a common grave,
And buried tyrants 'neath Oblivion's wave !

Hail bright improvement ! let the nations sing,
And some fair tribute **to thine altar bring;**
Yes, let us sing, 'tis the progressive mood
To **bow to** everything not understood;
To **live at** ease, as always dreamers do;
If others dream, let us be dreaming too;
Change **as** they change, their systems all approve;
Slay what they hate, and worship what they love;
Hail every Jehu who ascends the car,
Believe each Ignus Fatuus is a star;
Declare this light is brighter than the past,
And yield divinest honors to the **last;**
Find each possessing some magician spell,
And wait **on** tiptoe for a miracle !

Nor wait we long, nor ever wait in vain,
Ten thousand rise our wondering gaze to gain.

To-day 'tis Gall, and unto Gall we cleave,
To-morrow Gall and Spurzeim, too, we leave;
To-day we follow at the heels of Combe,
Or after Fowler or O'Lerey roam!
Forever seeking what is strange and new,
Another name will make the same thing do.
'Tis all progression, yet 'tis passing strange,
That half our progress is but love of change;
That words alone, if they be obsolete,
On placards posted quaintly round the street,
Tinged with some glaring color; green or blue,
No matter what, if white be not the hue;
Will draw together sinner, saint, and sage,
With all the wisdom of our boasted age,
To list in awe, in silent reverie,
To spirit rapping and phrenology;
Disclose what nature would have done for man,
Had priestly something not opposed the plan;
For now his native impulses are thwarted
By Education, and by creeds distorted;
Since still poor blinded, wonder-loving man,
Must worship something which he cannot scan,
And hide the beams of Nature's light beneath
A bigot's cowl, the sepulchre of truth,
Where Superstition rears her gloomy fane,
And countless, nameless, endless follies reign!

" Oh woman! in our hour of ease or pain,"
Won't now apply; sweet poet, try again—

When pain and anguish gather round the brow.
Revised edition, thus it readeth now ;
Oh lawless spirits, hither sent to tease !
Betimes to flatter, spoil our hours of ease ;
To make us dream a while of distant joy,
Then with a whisper all that bliss destroy.
Free from the rigid laws of right and wrong,
In thought, in deed, in feeling and in tongue ;
Free to encompass with delusive art,
Their latest victim, and ensnare the heart ;
And breathe on him their love and smiles together,
Then leave their trusting dupe and seize another !

Such were the rights to them by Nature left,
Though now by bigots of those rights bereft ;
Yes, plundered foully of what Nature gave,
And made of man the drudge, the dupe, the slave ;
Doomed to forego the rights once all their own,
And love and worship but with one alone.*

Nor would less blessings be to man restored,
The pride of earth, Creation's mighty lord ;
Though now degraded is that godlike form,
And sunk, his majesty, beneath the worm.
Yet 'twas not so by Nature's mild decree,
Man was created only to be free.
Then, wherefore, law, with marriage mockery bind
The free impulses of that master mind ?†

---

*It used to be a favorite maxim of the advocates of the Free Love doctrine, that the marriage contract was binding only while it satisfied both parties.

† "Washington, with his high intellect and noble moral character, ought to have been the father of a hundred sons," was taught by the advocates of advanced Socialism years ago.

Should fangled codes of **any** form control,
The inward promptings of that noble soul ?
'Twere weak to ask ; man was created free,
To reach the goal of moral destiny.

O ! glorious dreams of an **enlightened** age,
And glorious dreamers whom those dreams engage !
What high refinement **must give** birth **to** these,
What high **refinement they come forth to** please ;
How pure morality and common sense,
Must sit delighted 'neath such eloquence !
Nor e'en surmise **beneath its genial** flow,
The floods of dark iniquity below.

Is this the honored light from Science brought ?
The golden gleanings from the fount of thought ?
Which promise peace and love, and bliss below,
And ought with age emit a **brighter** glow ;
Or is it but the course of folly run,
In madness ending, **visions so begun ?**
Launching the soul on doubt's unsettled wave,
And sinking Faith and Hope beneath the grave,
Leaving the bosom but a heartless void,
With all its secret happiness destroyed.
O **guard us** angels ! grant us power to shun,
Those sin-born ravings of degenerate man,
Who would the trammell'd soul's deliverer be,
From Superstition's night, and moral lethargy ;
Who would the spirit's wings of thought unfold,
And plume her pinions with undrossy gold,
To sink or soar, as passion rose or fell,
In sight of heaven, but never far from hell !

If here lies truth or light, we **ask** no more ;
To us again our ignorance restore,
Restore again our follies to our breast,
If this be knowledge, ignorance is best !

Hush bats **and** vampires ! **to your** grottos **creep,**
Your day is o'er, 'tis time ye were asleep ;
Your sway must end, your throne to earth be trod,
Nor vice, nor virtue, heed your drowsy **nod** ;
Celestial messengers now cross death's tide,
And back and forth, runs **beaten pathway wide** !

O hail, bright spirits ! furtive glances cast,
To epochs o'er, to ages of the past,
Reveal how much to the decree we owe,
That leaves you now our sojourners below,
Clad in the brightness of your higher sphere,
And yielding all its heavenly radiance here.
'Twas a bold thought, that gather'd from the air,
The fiery current lawless flashing there ;
But bolder still the energies that laid
A cable down through Death's dark gloomy shade.
Now bearing here its messages sublime,
From the far regions 'yond the bounds of Time ;
Disclosing to us habitants below,
Some things we don't and some we wish to know ;
Nor leave that mystery of all untold
Of unwed ladies, **rap it out—how old** !

Celestial visitants ! our gratitude
Should bless, at least, this universal good ;
Hail in each rap, a revelation sent,
And to each medium raise a monument !

Ah ! when our sires would longingly look through
The veil that hid the death-land from their view,
Their fruitless efforts ended in despair,
And all their wishes in this hopeless prayer:
" Tell us ye dead, in pity let us see,
What 'tis ye are, and we must shortly be ;
But 'tis no matter, what the grave conceals,
An hour not distant to us all reveals."

Dear Jonathan, how much to thee we owe,
Debts long uncancelled on thy ledger show ;
Our endless catalogue of heavy bills,
For love-tales, anodynes, and patent pills ;—
For wise discoveries, which your forests yield,
And healing balms from herbage of the field,
Which meet Death's armies—Chilblains and Scrofula,
Proving Columbia, the land of Beulah,
Of which you happily retain the centre,
Where Death would be immortal should he enter.
Again, to remedy our special ills,
You are importers, well you know the pills
Whose claims to patronage the fair relate;
" And all but ladies in a certain state,"
That is, if married, otherwise the treasure
Is unrestrained, and all may act their pleasure.
O ! timely hint ! how modest and discreet
Is Virtue worshipping at Mammon's feet,—
How pure her aims, how wise the counsel given,
How like her portals to the gates of Heaven !

Illustrious quacks ! and newspaper physicians,
Half poets, conjurors, and politicians,

Whose friendly counsels all delight to meet,
Beneath your portrait on each village street ;
Where sunken eyes, dry phiz, and hollow cheeks,
Meet rustic notions of old thinking Greeks.
O ! happy day for you and for the people,
Which makes your wares as public as the steeple :
Yet some wear wrinkles, nurse an aching tooth,—
They fear your founts of everlasting youth :
They fear your power might make your promise true,
And give the world another Wandering Jew !
And rather take their chance through Hades' portals,
Than face the thought of joining the immortals !

Ah, well ! you have your dupes,—the press is paid,
And 'tis elysium for a love-sick maid,
Or youth, to fall upon your bright effusions,
And find hope revel even in delusions ;
While the mistaken sufferer dreams he sees
A brighter morn in promises like these :
Ho ! read afflicted ! a new wondrous book,
As medical adviser, or a cook ;
The pocket Esculapius for man;
Or, every one his own physician.
The Guide to Marriage ; gentlemen, take heed,
Think not of matrimony till you read !
Much of the ills and woes of married life
Come from your ignorance about a wife !
A book for ladies, specially designed,
Wherein the nursery duties are defined
In a familiar, interesting style,
With colored illustrations in profile,

And woodcuts, showing to the latest date,
New swaddling bands adopted by the great,
Meant to improve the figure, health and stature,
And all according to the laws of Nature.

O ! stupid age, in which our fathers flourished,
How could they thrive amid such darkess nourished ?
How did they find a mistress, or a trade,
And know so little of the heart and head ?
How did they ever come alive to earth,
Or e'en survive a moment after birth ?
When nought remains, not e'en their doctor's bills,
To show the world what genius made their pills !

Dear Brother Jonathan, 'tis not so now ;
A marked improvement meets us, you allow.
See Radway, with his pestle and his bowl,
And Ayer display his serpent on a pole,
The latter waiting to dispel our grief,
The former always ready with relief.
See others, only sparely clad in skins,
With miser noses reaching for their chins ;
Not vainly pictured so, though gin and toddy
Have done what we ascribe to lengthen'd study ;
That during thirty years of meditation
Upon the troubles which infest the nation,
They have forgotten fashion, so we take it,
And, in their innocence, that they are naked.
These are the hosts who thwart the King of Terrors,
Revive our joys, in spite of youthful errors,*

---

* I believe the suggestiveness of such advertisements often creates
the very evils they profess to cure.

And for our dimes—ah, there the magic power is—
Revive our dreams of Paradise and Houries!

'Tis, Jonathan, the order of the day
To advertise, and even devils may
Display their wares before the public gaze,
For who would advocate a muzzled press?
In this bright age when present to our view,
Are ocean cables, Spiritual, too;
And great Harmonicas, which tell how souls
Effect their exits through a vault's key holes.
Well we may now by some progressive beadle,
Find out if angels perch upon a needle,
And in what numbers,—little, if the sages
Should solve the mysteries of darker ages!

Dear Jonathan, great thoughts take greatest flights,
And mighty bonfires dim the lesser lights;
We know the wisdom of our fathers' days,
Must all be hidden in our noontide blaze;
Ours are high themes, and bearing sheaves along,
Ten thousand pilgrims swell the savant throng,
Which, if divided in pretence or name,
Is one in spirit, in effect the same;
Now entertaining visits from above,
Explaining now the art of making love!*

O, our poor sires! how did you ever know
How to succeed, and not to Rondout go?

---

* One Jared Lake, of New York, wrote a book: "The Art of Making Love," which was popular a quarter of a century ago.

How many stupid blunders did you make,
Avoided now by reading Jared Lake ?
How many harmless pleasantries, whose uses
And half-told hints from Venus and the muses,
Which might have saved you many a wakeful night ?
We now enjoy a national birthright,
But then your courtships little had of love,
Perhaps your drawing-room was but a grove ;
Your carpet may have only been the sod,
Your statues trees, and not the wingèd god.
Perhaps a grassy bank your seat at noon,
Your lamp at night not Luna, but the moon ;
Perhaps your hoidens romped about the hills,
And lived in cottages and drank from rills ;
While wild flowers only graced their lawless hair,
And home-spun skirts showed feet and ankles bare.
With these, whose fancies free and lawless rove,
What need to learn the art of making love ?
No, sweet coy shepherdess, who lead'st thy flocks
By the loud torrent from thy native rocks,
He who would woo thee, needs no other art
Than love's sweet theme, and language of the heart.
No sharpened arrows brought from Greece or Troy,
Go burn his bow, and hang the wingèd boy !

Dear envied belles, whose sentimental faces,
Are made to please when set in gilded cases ;
Whose fairy forms adorned in golden fleeces,
Must move just so, or else they go to pieces ;
Whose fancies keep you in a reign of terror,
Whose lives are sighs and curtsies to the mirror ;

Whose tiny feet in silken slippers pent,
Are not to walk, but just for ornament ;
Whose faithful lovers' coveted rewards,
Speak modestly from conversation cards.
Celestial nymphs who only live and bloom,
Within the desert of the drawing-room.
What priceless boons to you the gods have brought,
On which your mothers never spent a thought ?
What wealth of beauty could the heart desire,
Not now bestowed by Boswell's Beautifier ?
Could Venus' girdle have imparted more,
Than you possess in Roland's Kalydor ?
To make you both a phantasy and dream,
Love's new compound of strawberries and cream.
On which lorn hearts in silent rapture gaze,
With love fast changing from a smoke to blaze !
O'er which fast knave both well and wisely nurses
His love for you, but always plus your purses !
Alas ! fair nymphs, 'tis pity your ideal,
Should lose itself, and in so tame a real.

Dear Jonathan, our theme is somewhat sad,
And somewhat laughable by folly made ;
Your sanguine hopes predict that wrong shall cease,
" Men's virtues with their knowledge will increase."
Almost an axiom, Jonathan, I know,
But often doubt if time will prove it do.
Man's a strange animal, and what he would be,
In other state, and even what he could be,
We cannot tell. By love attracted here,
And driven there by hate, despair, and fear.
" He vibrates still between a smile and tear."

Usher'd he is into a world of trouble,
And countless woes which discontent must double.
With all life's dread reality of sorrow,
Insatiate still, and ever prone to borrow;
His griefs on hand are seldom found enough,
He adds thereto imaginary stuff
His lighter ills may flee a draught of tansy,
But how dislodge the devils of his fancy ;
And those by heirdom with his being blended,
As spleen or gout, from hundred Earls descended.
They leave him not for Brunn or Baden waters,
Nor forest wines nor everlasting bitters,
They follow, follow like unlucky games,
Which find a lethe in the Seine or Thames,
Or haunt him still, till life's last moment flies,
A life-long pilgrim on the bridge of sighs.

Well, Jonathan, I find the hour is late,
And now to thee, this strain I dedicate.
Perhaps 'tis tame, but yet upon reflection,
May point some matters that require correction,
Before we start upon our final trip,
From Sandy Hook, on the millennial ship.
I say this all, with feelings of a brother,
And tell thee much, I would not tell another,
For I do love thee.   Though John Bull, a donkey,
Can never see how Adam was a Yankee ;
Yet ere we part, permit one short quotation,
We both admit you are a mighty nation,
And that your eagle is a mighty creature,
The greatest Dodo ever found in nature ;

A glorious bird ; in fact, a seventh wonder ;
From tip to tip expansive as a condor ;
And thus enabled with a swoop gigantic,
To reach from the Pacific to Atlantic,
When on the Rocky Mountains set, its beak,
Set north or nearly, gazing from Pike's Peak,
It reaches up to the Mackenzie River,
And preys upon the stragglers from Vancouver !
While, spreading out its length the other way,
Its tail sweeps graceful o'er the Mexique Bay ;
And there it sits, your joys and hopes to nourish,
And hatch your niggers, bid your freedom flourish;
And guard your virtues with a jealous eye,
Extending everything that ends in Y.
Hence Jonathan, your *liberty*, and *glory*,
And all such things as *money, territory.*
This last has made our heroes think if whether
They should not get their old flint locks together ;
And rusty swords, which have not seen a fight,
Since last they flourished them at Queenston Height.
Ah well ! Dear Jonathan, that fight is o'er,
And pray we God, that we shall fight no more ;
But if the future finds your flag unfurled,
We hope to stand with you against the world ;
The Union Jack, the Stars and Stripes, and we
Shall join our little ensign, making three.
Who reasons ask, shall find to axle grease,
That we are ready, be it war or peace.
'Tis midnight bells.   The moon has veiled her light,
My song is sung, Dear Jonathan, good night !

SONG FOR THE SAD

Written after the siege of Lucknow.

WHEN the loud trump of war breaks the slumber of nations,
And wrests from the peasant the peace he enjoys,
How harsh are the plaudits, how poor **the oblations,**
Which Glory bestows for the bliss she destroys ?

Though **joy** might arise from the shout 'yond the ocean,
Proclaiming success to **the arm of the** brave,
The rapture is lost in **the tide of** emotion
That **wakes** for the **thousands who find** but a grave.

When princes **exult** o'er the daring **of heroes,**
And kings condescend **their** successes **to praise,**
'Twere joy could the heralds **of** victory spare us
The low, **saddened murmur that** springs from **the vale.**

From the vale where the victims **of war had** delighted
The pleasures of **love and of friendship to share ;**
Alas ! when they sleep and their homes are benighted,
Will glory **bring joy** to **the** heart-stricken there ?

Will glory enliven the grot by the fountain
Where Mary would fain meet her lover again,—
Would hope that ere spring has spread flowers o'er the
        mountain,
His arms may embrace her,—would hope, but in vain !

For far from his kindred, unknown and neglected,
His **corse** uninterred must be left on the plain ;
While only the fame of the triumph effected,
Shall e'er reach his home **or** his Mary again.

Can glory, on her who is lonely lamenting
The sire of her children, contentment bestow ?
Will grief for the tinsel of gold be relenting ?
Or Fame bring a balm for the torture of woe ?

Ah, no ! with her home seeming cold, lone and dreary,
She lingers awhile to bereavement a prey ;
And silently weeps, like poor heart-broken Mary,
Till called from the scenes of her sadness away.

Yet onward, ye brave ! seize e'en passing glory !
If all but the phantom the price should destroy,
The winds shall waft home to old Scotland your story,
'Tis all ye can leave the bereft to enjoy.

'Tis all, when invasion or tyranny gathers
Your sons to oppose, or their rights to maintain,
Can wake in their bosoms a soul like their fathers,
To act o'er the deeds ye have acted again !

LOVE IN A COTTAGE.

Love built a cottage, when the heart was young,
Beside a hill, not distant from the shore,
No cumbrous trappings round the dwelling hung,
No superfluities of wealth it bore.
Not there had Art her boasted labors spent
On sculptured capitals or marble walls,
And scarce but Nature any beauty lent
To the chaste beauty of its snowy halls.

Wherein no Raphael nor Rubens hung,
Yet to supply the want (if such it were),
Around its portals warm May blossoms clung,
As if they loved and lived to flourish there.
And clinging vines, by careful culture made
To furnish all that taste or fancy loves,
And fruit and flower around profusely shed
The pleasing fragrance of Italian groves.

Not downy couches, tempting to repose
A wakeful conscience, formed its inmates' bed,
Whose weariness was not from wants or woes
By vice, ambition or indulgence made,
But from glad hours in healthful labor spent,
Which ready opiate seals the peasants' eyes,
Who, blessed with vigor, innocence, content,
To meet the morn refreshed and happy rise.

Not there had Fashion spread her subtle wiles,
But bland Contentment, from her ampler store,
Bestow'd her favors with a thousand smiles,
Nor left a longing, nor created more.
And yet, unfailing as the seasons' round,
Were countless joys and pleasures ever new,
Among the number of her favors found,
Profusely lavish'd on a faithful few.

Who, oft unknown in circles of the great,
Partake unmeasured of that purer joy,
Which, 'mid the dull satiety of state,
Not long can flourish or is ever coy.

Though Heaven, impartial, every gift bestow,
Yet seldom meeting 'neath the lordly dome,
Such peace and happiness untainted flow
As knew the inmates of this cottage home.

Before whose portals, pleased, the noonday sun,
Half lingering, waits his brightest smiles to shed,
And morn's first music of the grove begun,
Calls flow'ry spring her richest gems to spread.
Here, less for magnitude than beauty known,
A spreading vale where Ceres' bounties grew
In all the promise of the season shone,
Inspiring hope and yielding pleasure too.

And near in view the valley gently rose,
And formed into a mildly sloping hill,
Where evening zephyrs latest sought repose,
And from its bosom flowed a gentle rill.
Where earth's first fruits, to life and beauty sprung,
And summer's berries grew, inviting, cool,
Where fruitful autumn on the hazel hung
Hoards for the vagrants of a neighb'ring school.

And, brook-encircled, out in richness spread
A verdant holm where herds were left to stray,
Which Edwin's labors through the winter fed,
But Nature feasted each returning May.
When Emma's toils—too welcome to be care—
Amid her flocks at early dawn begun,
Pleased of the grove the waking song to share,
And join the latest to the setting sun.

Here Edwin dwelt from fancied sorrows free,
Unknown to avarice or want's alarms,
Blest in possessing health and liberty,
And happy monarch of young Emma's charms,
Whose artless beauty, to herself unknown,
A warmth and sweetness to its magic lent,
Which now, from faith and love diviner grown,
Diffused a grace o'er every lineament.

And here, to strengthen all that love endears,
Approving Heaven the choicest blessings sent,
When happy Emma, mingling hopes and fears,
Knew all the raptures to glad mothers lent.
And Edwin, too, with unaffected joy,
Few moments knew like those when left to trace
In kindling features of their infant boy
The radiant beauty of his Emma's face.

Oh, happy Emma! happy, happy pair!
Unknown to all the vanities of life,
Unknown to pangs of self-created care,
And sordid Mammon's never-ending strife.
Remote from cities in your humble hall,
All-bounteous Nature every want supplies,
Nor heed what empire may arise or fall,
What sage may flourish or what monarch dies.

Yet not to hopeless ignorance consigned,
For Edwin mystic science has a charm,
Rich in the native energies of mind,
Chaste in desire, although in feeling warm.

Some patriot bard to claim his evening hours
Among the treasures of his home remains,
A lute, from which the sweetest music pours
When Emma's voice can mingle with its strains.

Oh sacred happiness! too little known,
Too oft unvalued, for a bauble lost;
For gold, ambition, or an empty name,
For gilded greatness, worthlessness at most,
Which ever fails to yield the promised joys,
Or fancied pleasure, impotent to bless :
Familiarity the glare destroys,
And leaves their value by possession less.

But gold, like other dust, in Edwin's eyes,
Ambition too, had little but the name,
Unless from Emma, often ling'ring nigh,
To **gain** approval, happly waked the flame.
Nor could he learn wherein the greatness lies,
Whose highest merit springs from birth **alone,**
Or bought perchance for sycophantic praise,
Bestowed or barter'd round a monarch's throne,—

Where Edwin's thoughts had never sought to rove,
Nor Emma's fancy e'er excursions made,
Rich in the joys of undivided love,
Not purer found than in their cottage shade ;
Where not to monarchs were they forced to bow,
Who, of a titled majesty bereft,
And the vain trappings of a gaudy show,
May have but little to commend them left.

But nobler far, unto the King of Kings,
In glad allegiance they submissive bend,
To Him their earliest morning anthem springs,
And evening's latest songs of praise ascend,
On which their souls in bless'd communion rise ;
And, for a season leaving earth behind,
Faith to the home of many mansions flies,
Where faith and hope their full fruition find.

Where all their higher joys converging meet,
Where every care is banished from the breast,
Where love aspires to happiness complete,
Within the city of eternal rest.
Where strife, and pain, and **earth-born troubles** cease,
And Mammon's all absorbing sway is o'er,
Where reigns the once rejected Prince of Peace,
Where earthly monarchs study war no more.

Such were the hopes that lighted Edwin's breast,
In which his Emma equal transports knew ;
Hopes left by years untarnished to the last,
Which brighter flourished as they older grew.
Such was the wealth the changing seasons brought,
As on they floated down the stream of time ;
Such were the joys with highest promise fraught,
Which Faith had treasured in a better clime.

To mete with these the lauded joys how vain,
Or envied pleasures of the worldly great,
Whose short-lived revelry oft ends in pain,
Whose stores of wealth, but cares accumulate.

And for the vaunted greatness they bestow,
Or envied glitter they awhile control,
Impose perchance an equal weight of woe,
Or blast the nobler feelings of the soul!

Then what is all that riches ever brought?
The giddy joy, the flowery wreath of fame?
The dark creations of misguided thought?
Ambition's prize, the magic of a name?
But visions, baseless, cold, that cannot yield
To their possessors happiness supreme,
When "vanity of vanities" revealed,
Leave but the phantoms of life's fitful dream,

That lure along the power-enamoured train
Of monarchs, heroes, conquerors and kings;
Who reap their harvest in the guilt and pain,
At the last goal, which disappointment brings!
Where dark despair counts o'er the seasons lost,
With dire compunction gnawing at the breast,
Or broods in silence o'er the troubled past,
O'er pander'd innocence, and vanished rest.

Then hail, sweet peace! and flourish, humble cot,
Where Edwin early waked to meet the morn;
Long may contentment please him with his lot,
Long may his breast remain by care untorn.
And long may Emma know unsullied joy,
Through all the changes of life's shifting scene;
May no rude blast the happiness destroy,
Of joyous Edwin's graceful cottage queen.

And hail, mild joys! that glad life's lowly train,
Long, long, may Spring her verdant beauty spread
Around their dwellings, Summer's sun and rain
Enlarge their stores, and Autumn yield them bread.
And as they journey towards life's setting sun,
As one by one time's passing beauties fade;
Be still their bosoms as when life begun,
Like flowers still fragrant when the bloom's decay'd.

And hand in hand may they together go
Up o'er the summit, down life's sunset hill.
When, travel-wasted, weary, worn and slow,
May faith, and love, and hope, grow brighter still.
O fair, fair cottage by the woodland set,
With grateful shade, sweet peace, and azure sky,
Long may love flourish in thy mild retreat,—
I say, farewell! but leave thee with a sigh!

THE HAPPY DAYS OF OLD.

Dear Wifie, back o'er thirty years,
I trace Time's rapid onward flow,
Still would I, with its pains and tears,
Live o'er again our long ago:
For I have gather'd by the way,
Perhaps some glitter, but some gold,
And still would have my treasure stay,
From those bright, happy days of old.

Dear little wifie by my side,
I often look when you don't know,
And think you still my joy and pride,
As in the days of long ago.
O, Love is ever, ever young !
His willing worship never cold ;
Devotion flows from heart and tongue,
As in the happy days of old.

Dear wifie, seasons change and shift,
The old depart, **the** younger grow,
With here and there a relic left,
As **you and I,** from long ago.
Time writes his record o'**er the face** ;
But though by cheek and eye **'tis told,**
The heart is still love's dwelling place,
As in the happy days **of old.**

Dear wifie, we have fashions met,
And cross'd, **each seventh** year or so ;
But true hearts are in fashion yet,
As we had found them long ago.
And through our toils Hope lightens **care** ;
No change in this the years unfold,
Hope is **in season** everywhere,
As in the happy days of old.

Dear wifie, bang nor bustle yet,
Nor tresses frizz'd, had you to show ;
Back from your pure, brave brow they set,
As in the days of **long** ago.

THE HAPPY DAYS OF OLD.

If through those tresses winters' chill
Have woven silver in their fold,
Love holds within his mirror still,
The tresses of the days of old!

Dear little wifie, youth has fled,
And that means much, so much you know,
When mem'ry feeds upon the dead
But happy days of long ago!
Yet though 'tis pleasure dull'd with pain,
Our joys are often still retold;
We taste the hours of bliss again,
We knew in happy days of old.

We had not wealth of gold nor lands,—
Just love, with little else to show;
But then, brave hearts and willing hands
Were counted something long ago.
We waited not for wealth to come,
Till hearts grew faint and love grew cold,
But built in faith and hope our home
In those bright, happy days of old.

We wore the cloths our mothers spun.
The cut or fashion?   Not for show,
But they were in the fashion then,
When we were lovers, long ago.
We gather'd at the rustic ball,
None heeded distance, storm, nor cold,
For youth could change to summer all
The winter storms of long ago!

We wander'd home beneath the stars,
Across the pure, untrodden snow ;
If time has left us wounds and scars,
They cannot hide that long ago.
Your hand lay trustingly in mine—
The glove unneeded, may be told,
For heart or hand has not been thine
Since that bright, happy night of old.

Those Heaven has planted round our hearth,
In love and joy we've seen them grow;
And watch'd with pride their truth and worth,
And bless the days of long ago !
And though we have affliction tried,
The fire that purifies the gold
Has left our hearts e'en more allied
Than in the happy days of old.

Our tears have mingled o'er our dead,
That silent lie beneath the snow,
We death's pale flowers of anguish spread
Above their graves, long, long ago !
And now we only stand and wait
Till life's last solemn hour is tolled,
But cherish to the latest date,
The happy, happy days of old !

WAYFARERS.

DARLING, sitting by my side,
While the shadows longer grow,—
Fearing, waiting, by the tide;
Shrinking **from** the hour to go.

Hither, **up** from love's **bright** morn,
We have travelled hand **in** hand;
One alone must cross the **bourn**,
One stand weeping on **the strand.**

Like the millions gone before,
Each must pass into **the** night;
Outward to the silent shore,
Only hoping for the light!

In the future yet to be,
Darkness, **death** and doubting o'er,
Shall you, darling, wake with me,
Earth's sad longings felt no more.

Or shall we there, as here, enquire?—
Find there still a vast unknown?
Has that world, though purer, higher,
Still some mystery of its own?

SUNSET ON LAKE MANITOU.

COME some wizard power,
Bid the cloudlets rest,
Bind the sun an hour,
In the golden west.

Stay the dying day,
Catch the evening song;
While the zephyrs play,
Bear the notes along.

Drive the shuttles pale,
That from beams of light,
Weave a silver veil
O'er the waters bright.

By the margin still,
Where the ripples meet,
Catch with painter's skill,
Children lave their feet.

Calm the thoughts that rise
From a soul's despair;
Voice the hope that sighs
Through a maiden's prayer.

If she idly rove,
If the heart be sear,
If she dream of love,
May it not be here?

Amy by my side,
Dry those tears I see ,
When this world so wide,
Holds but you and me !

Gazing in thy face,
In those eyes so blue,
This **is not the** place,
For a sigh from you.

Sorrow near or far,
Cannot reach us here ;
Neither **peace nor war,**
Brings us joy or **fear.**

Here we **have no** past ;
To-morrow's clouded brow
Here no shadows cast,—
There is only now !

Weep you since the flowers
Only last a day ?
In this world of ours,
Nothing comes to stay

Altar touched with fire,
From the torch of Heaven,
Flames not brighter, higher,
Than the moment given.

Shrines our souls may frame,
Where we incense burn,
Will not be the same,
If we do return !

Yet from **deepest pain,**
Purest joys we kiss;
Through what years remain,
We shall turn to this.

E'en the evening grey
Of life's sinking powers
Cannot steal away
This bright day of ours!

List the tinkling bell
On the rocky height!
See! adown the dell,
Creep the shades of night.

Spectre forms awake,
Move among the trees;
O'er the sleeping lake,
Sighs the **dying** breeze.

Darkness **deepens o'er,**
Lamps **of heaven are** lit;
On the farther shore,
Night-born phantoms flit.

Silent lips must take
Here our heart's adieu!
Out into the **lake**
Glides my bark canoe!

WAITING.

By the dark ocean of the silent shore,
Of which we know along the hither side,
But one small inlet, where the stranded soul
Was drift ashore, to earth's captivity ;
To chafe throughout the hours, and days, and years,
Of time's probation, it is left to fill,
In mute rebellion 'gainst its exiled state ;
Dashing itself against its prison bars,
Till torn and broken with the bootless strife,
It takes the hue and form of earthly things,
And sinks to dumb endurance of its fate :
As monarch eagle of his pinions shorn,
And vainly longing for his wastes of air,
Must feed on carrion he would else despise ;
Or like wrecked sailor on his barren isle,
Treading the sand with weary, noiseless step,
With longing glances cast across the tide,
To meet but phantoms, whence no answering call,
Or echo ever to the shore returns.
So, on life's narrow isthmus where we stand,
To all the spirit's longing that goes forth,
No voice from out the eternal darkness comes
To calm this busy seething scene of man,
Till the poor famished soul must feed on husks
Of gold, or fame, or crude philosophy,
Or piety in party-colored vest,
That kills the spirit, wears its longing out,
And builds its heaven on this narrow shore ;
Till, looking upward to the silvery stars,

The soul's drown'd senses hear no voice that calls
Adown the long and silent lanes of blue ;
But sinks in drowsy lethargy in death,
To rise reanimate no more in time !

TOO LATE.

THEY met, seemed by chance, in a green shady by-way,—
A fragrant oasis where pilgrims might rest ;
Remote one short stage, back from life's dusty highway,
Where day folds his wings, as he sinks in the west.
He was worn, for the travail of years had gone o'er him,
His garments were faded, his sandals were torn ;
The desert stretch'd cheerless behind and before him,
And Hope gave no promise to brighten the morn !

She was young, and more fair than the vision that frightens
A saint at his prayer, when an angel comes down ;
And pure as the angel that gladdens and brightens,
The poor homes of earth ere receiving her crown.
God made her the fairest and best of His creatures,
Gave a heart for the temple of worship and love,
And moulded her form, and chiselled her features,
From model the seraphs might envy above !

Her eyes were the blue of the calm evening heaven,
When washed by a shower, and the sunlight breaks through,
And the light, and the calm, and the tear-drops are given,
To kindle, and brighten, and soften the blue.

On her lips was a smile, that had followed from childhood;
The pure blush of girlhood gave warmth to her cheek.
From her heart rose the soft, sighing notes of the wildwood,
Like zephyrs and sunshine in music that speak.

Thus she stood in the dawn, 'twixt life's springtime and
    summer,
The child fast departing, the woman in view.
With her joys, and her cares, and her hopes come upon her
All waiting in tears to bid girlhood adieu !
So they met all alone 'neath a palm in the desert,
To rest for the night, and to wait for the morn :—
He old, with his life's dream of love still in his heart,
She young, with its joy and its pain still unborn.

Hers the face and the form for which his soul hunger'd,
His boyhood and manhood in visions had seen :
His heart's dream of joy, o'er which mem'ry linger'd
Through hope's sad refrain, of what life might have been.
And he gazed on the vision that God set before him,—
The pure, and the young, and the bright, and the fair ;
And a fear and a joy, and a silence came o'er him,
Love's last fateful striving 'twixt hope and despair !

Then his hair which was grey, flashed the hue of the raven;
From his face pass'd the traces of age and of pain ;
And the locks on his forehead were glossy and waven,—
He just for a moment touched boyhood again.
Then his brain struck a chord on the border of madness,
His heart beat the pulses his manhood had known ;
And the red tide of life roll'd in torrents of gladness,
Along the worn channels, their youth had outgrown !

He arose, from her brow raised the soft, silken tresses,
On her pure maiden lips press'd a lover's warm kiss,
But no blush on her cheek rose to meet his caresses,
No sigh from her heart for a rapture like this.
Then he **knew** only youth can be mated with beauty,
That manhood **and** strength seize the young **and the fair,**
And he laid **his dead heart on** the altar of **duty,**
And crushed through his teeth the low wail of despair !

Then the blackness of darkness hung pall-like before him,
And paradise closed while he stood at the **gate,**
And the death-sigh of hope like a spirit passed o'er him,
And moaned through the silence, " Too late !   Ah, **too**
    late ! "
Here, standing alone with his life's love unspoken,
O'er his face passed a shadow the gods weep to **see,**
When the ashes of death were in silence unbroken,
Shed deep o'er the grave of a love could not be.

Thus he drained his deep cup from the waters of Mara,
And fierce o'er his soul drove despair's chilling **blast,**
On the cold wings of death from his life's bleak Sahara,
Where his cross had been borne and his Calvary passed.
So he laid himself down, but the Death-wave returning.
Passed o'er him, too weary and broken to weep,
But he slept, **and the** songs and the music of morning
Disturbed not his dreaming and broke not his **sleep.**

But she wandered away to the land of the summer,
To gather the flowers that were strewn in her way,
And reck'd not the love amid life's glare and glamor,
Of the cold broken heart in the desert that lay.

Oh ! why but the apples of Sodom that perish
We gather from life's long devotion and pain ?
For the love and the faith which our hearts fondly
    cherish,
Why only the husks and the ashes remain ?

QUESTIONINGS.

FORTY years' ago to-night,
Toss'd about like ocean spray ,
From the wings of time alight,
On the shore a bubble lay !

Bubble or immortal soul,
Reached the ecstacy of pain ;—
Touch'd at matter's highest goal,
To return to dust again.

Down the cycling ages come,
Whence the lines converging meet,
Lords from pale Ascidians dumb,
Or the oysters now they eat !

Souls are sublimated clay,—
Strange affinities of earth,
Mixed and mingled on their way
Upward to a spirit's birth.

In the transit,—**clod to** thought,
Conscience, Sin and Death are born,
And their doubting children brought,—
Firstlings of terrestrial morn.

Then, the " clouds of glory," all
Leave some question that abides,
Eternity is what ? **A pall !**
Time supplies **the** dead **it hides.**

Earth, the origin **and end,**
Who would, being, thence, explore,
Finds the path **through death extend**
To a sea without a shore !

Finds to Seraph Choir sublime,
Through each note an echo calls,—
" **Fate and** Chaos, Space **and Time,**
Lie without the jasper walls ! "

Questions may in heaven arise,—
There may be some grief to bear ;
Actions neither just nor wise,—
Choice and motive even there : *

Some high purpose to fulfil,
Worn-out worlds to build anew,—
Power and wisdom brooding still,
O'er the wisest thing to do.

---

* " And it **repented the** Lord **that** he had made man on the earth,
and it grieved **him at** his heart."—Gen. vi. 6.

Earth-born souls still higher, higher,
From their low estate to raise ;
Burnished through affliction's fire,
Ending in celestial praise !

AT THE CLOSE OF THE DAY.

HAIL ! **youth's** joyous dreaming,
With rainbow hues beaming,
To light up the steeps along life's rugged way,
Where the tracery lingers
Of Hope's fairy fingers,
Among the bleak peaks till the close of the day !

Though the schemes of ambition
May fail of fruition,
And honest endeavor seem scarcely to pay ;
Though poverty's canker,
And toil's pain and rancour,
Should darken our joys till the close of the day !

Still far down the valley,
The bright visions rally,—
Though Autumn belie all the promise of May,
Still come they intruding,—
On the weary heart brooding,—
Hope's oft broken vows, till **the** close of the day !

And all our sad yearning
O'er wisdom and learning,
And Fame, that still dallies in doubt and delay,

Finds life's sun, if shining,
Too surely declining,
In the dull, hazy West, at the close of the day.

And poor, waning beauty
Finds love changed to duty,
But not the devotion the heart used to pay
At the shrine of affection,
Where pale recollection
Gathers brown wither'd leaves at the close of the day !

And thus disenchanted,
The cheek is presented—
To claim the sweet tribute the lips used to pay !
Oh ! why should we ever
Awake to discover
Love vanish'd afar ere the close of the day !

Where Age thus has found us,—
The desert around us,
And gods we had worshipped turned idols of clay ;
We build our new altars,
Where faith fails and falters,
Though Hope follows still till the close of the day.

Here the praises are chanted
Of Duty, and vaunted,—
Her pale Arctic light, and her cold frigid ray ;
But oh ! to restore us
The light that shone o'er us
When youth took the path at the dawn of the day !

Our riches all seeming
All bright, golden dreaming;
Still wealth all enduring, if youth would but stay—
With past pain forgotten,
And ills that might threaten,
All banish'd afar till the close of the day.

Proud lord in his carriage,
Our lot might disparage;
We heeded him not, as we trudged on our way.
Youth's flowers were all wither'd,
Long, long, ere we gather'd,—
That death equals all at the close of the day!

Distinctions and stations,
We thought the oblations
Bestowed for the homage which fools had to pay;
By us not regarded,
For virtue rewarded,—
Her meed would be ours at the close of the day!

Fair motives to guide us,
With youth still beside us;
But wanting, with sorrow and sickness at bay,—
With age creeping o'er us,
And nothing before us
But toil, weary toil, till the close of the day!

A GRANDSIRE'S CHRISTMAS.

He dreaming sits in easy chair,
From wants and care's intrusion free,
Time's silvery frost-work through his hair,
His children's children by his knee ;
Gold's trophies round him, wealth and art,
Bright treasures of the head and heart,
But what awakes love's after glow,
Amid his sixty winters' snow ?

'Mid youth and mirth he sits alone,
'Tis distant music greets his ears ;
Long changed to softest monotone,
Through mellow cadence of the years.
'Tis other boys and other girls,
Touch auburn locks and golden curls ;—
The faces now that round him glow,
Are faces long beneath the snow !

O potent memory ! thine the power
That wakes the joys too sweet to last,
And centres in a single hour,
All the glad radiance of the past ;—
That trembles on the grandsire's lips,
And reaches to his finger tips ;
And brings him love's warm after-glow,
Amid his sixty winters' snow.

While all forgotten is the pain
That spread itself athwart the years ;
Ah ! is he not a boy again ?
And knows his happiness in tears.

He sees the little garden gate
Where he had lingered long and late,
And knows love's pure sweet after-glow,
Amid his sixty winters' snow.

Forgotten ! Yes, state, power, and gold,
Ambition's guerdon—vain regret,—
Tall windows drap'd in crimson fold,
And Parian vase and statuette ;
For when, from o'er the silent tide,
Beside him stands his spirit bride,
Not all of wealth and art bestow
The warmth that melts his winters' snow.

Bright clouds, distill'd from dews of morn,
Returned to clothe the sinking sun ;
For us so weary travel-worn,
Ye gild the day so nearly done ;
And in your " clouds of glory " trail,
Both orange flowers and bridal veil,
To deck in love's warm after-glow
The bleakness of our winters' snow.

Sweet, happy childhood! in your joys,
That bring to us the vanished past,
We feel again like girls and boys,
For one brief hour that cannot last.
Still let us for a moment dream,
And launch youth's bark on life's rough stream,
And watch it gliding, swift or slow,
Down through our sixty winters' snow.

How swiftly **pass life's** morning hours?
How more than swiftly those of age?
How soon the changing suns and showers
Shall leave but one unwritten page?
But those who from their **labors rest,**
With winter shroud above their breast,
Ah, do they see us? Will they know
We think of them beneath the snow?

EVENING.

STANDING by the **broken wall,**
Where the evening **shadows fall,**
And the drowsy night **birds call,**
    Far, far away!

Wither'd flower with broken stem,
Summer morning's dewy gem,
Old and feeling, I like them
    Have had my day!

Leafless grove and silent bower,
Beauty's charm and music's power,
Come to bless one fleeting hour,
    Then dark decay!

Youth would laugh and maiden sing
If 'twere always love and spring,
But they vanish, all take wing,
    Youth, love and May!

Dear ones slumber in the mould,
All the living grim and cold,
Gone together, gilt and gold,
    Why should I stay !

Time brings summer to a close,
Autumn into winter grows,
Cold beneath the silent snows,
    Death holds his sway !

One last thought to valleys green,
To sylvan lake in silver sheen,
The love and glory that have been,
    Then whence away ?

SHADOWS ON THE FLOOR.

SITTING in the evening twilight,
Watching phantoms at the door,
That, with spirit footsteps gliding,
Noiseless pass athwart the floor.
Pass with silent fingers weaving—
Weaving, through the waning light,
Webs of darker, deeper shadow,
Falling from the shroud of night.

Back and forth the shadows flutter ;
Mem'ry, through the deep'ning gloom,
Plies her swiftly flying shuttle,
Waking voices from the tomb,—

Calling back, in childhood's treble,
Through bereavement's lonely years,
Mingling woman's wail of anguish
With those bitter manhood's tears.

Weaving boyhood's love, so tender,
With his glowing dreams of bliss,
And his all-in-all of Eden,
Shatter'd in a world like this!
Weaving girlhood's song and sadness
With the woman's fuller joy,—
Reaching out to hope's hereafter,
All life's pain can not destroy.

Weaving through the changing seasons,
Spring, with bird, and song, and shower,
Summer, with its glow of glory,—
Life, and hope, and faith, and power.
Weaving still through slow gradations,
All the brightness Autumn sears;
Through the lengthen'd nights of sorrow,
Down the Winter of our years.

Weaving childhood, youth and manhood,
In the light of mem'ry's page,
With the broken shrines that meet us,
Through the pilgrimage of age.
Weaving, weaving, ever weaving,
From the writing on the wall,
Pictures which the coming morrow
Finds, if pale, not vanished all.

Weaving, weaving, ever weaving,
Ah, those phantoms by the door!
Which throughout the twilight watches,
Pass in silence o'er the floor.
God! Oh God! we cry, have mercy!
Must it thus for evermore?—
Is not love, nor youth, nor beauty,
Without shadows on the floor!

Long, so long, the shadows linger,
Dark, so dark, the weary night,
While the stricken heart lies waiting,—
Hoping for the morning light!
When the veil of darkness riven,
And the ghosts of mem'ry laid,
Glide, in vanquished pale battalions,
Backward to the realms of shade.

THE PUSLINCH LAKE.

The following beautiful poem was written some ten years ago by Mr.
Malcolm MacCormick, now Principal of the Guelph Business College.
My own effort in the same line was inspired by the memories which it
awoke. The two poems are, therefore, with Mr. MacCormick's per-
mission, published together.

AYE once again! O, silent, sylvan lake,
I stand upon thy verdant wave-plashed shore;
And cherished memories within me wake,
As I recall the halcyon days of yore.

Oft have my willing footsteps hither strayed,
Ere yet the glow of boyhood's years had fled ;
Ere yet the dreams of youth were rudely frayed,
Or loved companions numbered with the dead.

How fair the morn when from yon eastern hill
Thy waters greeted first my wondering sight ;
Thy radiant beauty made my bosom thrill
With the pulsations of a new delight.

The western breeze upon the ripples played,
That gaily sparkled on thy bosom fair ;
Thy island woods their graceful branches swayed,
And scattered fragrance on the morning air.

With eager hands we pushed the boat from shore,
That waiting lay upon the pebbly beach ;
My comrades twain took each a willing oar,
And forth we sped the island shades to reach.

In merry converse sped the happy hours,
No voice save Nature's mingled with our own ;
A joy that knew no touch of care was ours—
Ah ! why have boyhood's hours so quickly flown ?

But now the scene is changed, O sylvan lake !
And stately mansions sentinel thy shore;
Amid thy woods the slumbering echoes wake,
Responsive to the steamer's sullen roar.

'Tis evening, and o'er yon same eastern hill,
The rounded moon comes slowly into view ;
Her mellow splendor falling calm and still,
Bedecks with varied gems the waters blue

Dear are the scenes of childhood to the heart,
Deep their impressions stamped upon the mind;
Though earth's wide orb their presence from us part,
Fond mem'ry paints them still with pencil kind.

TO THE PUSLINCH LAKE POET.

DEAR POET of the Puslinch Lake,
You rove through youth's bright glades and dells;
And gather from each shady brake
Life's rare, sweet flowers—Heart Immortelles.

But as you back in mem'ry stray
O'er silent years, like moments fled,
You find **her album leaves are grey**
With ashes **of her buried dead!**

My memory, too, has held her wake
O'er empty shrouds of morning haze,
And, doubting, stands, what path to take
Along **life's** dim, forgotten *blaze.*[a]

For it is now so long ago
Since I youth's thoughtless paths have trod—
That I must **up the current row,**
Than you, a longer, rougher road.

---

[a] An axe mark on trees, by which travellers found their way through the forests in pioneer days,

I scarce dare write, " When we were boys,"
When fate gave sun with shadow mix'd,
And highest hopes and purest joys
Seem now old gold with drab betwixt.

But yet I know there was a time
When I had dreams, survived the night !
Heard echoes from a fairer clime,
Saw rays of pure though distant light !

I'll write it, yes—" When we were boys,"
Football and cricket, school days, these
Not heard of. No, our early joys
Were *ax-e-dents* in felling trees.

Toil's vassals have so small a range
In youth, or age in change of toys,
But still has come to me a change,
At least in pounds avoirdupois.

Well, I have seen your " sylvan lake,"
Where caught I gudgeons not a few,
But found, alas ! the finny take,
Like other friends were spiny, too !

I've paddled by your bullrush shore,
That ne'er beyond its calfhood grew ;
'Twas only paddle *then*, not oar,
A dug-out navy all *we* knew :

Till rose a pious Teuton, who
Resolved to build a boat, and took
The model for his big canoe
From somewhere in the Pentateuch.

Her beamage,—broad as ancient barn,
She thereunto of equal height;
And somewhat longer than my yarn,—
'Twas said,—about a coach and eight.

She was, indeed, a wondrous craft,
And nautically rated **thus** :—
Her *aft* was *fore*, her *fore* was *aft*,
Her tonnage *minus*, leakage *plus*.

She had a pump with deck to show,
Between the waters firmly fixed,
And, just a little space below,
The lake and hold were badly mix'd

She tried one voyage, ran aground,
With dire misfortune in her wake :
The pump was tax'd, but soon 'twas found
'Twere wiser first to pump the lake.

So thus the Teuton's venture bore
That sad, sad fruit, " what might have been : "—
One voyage only, and no more,
Then left to rot in quarantine !

Yes, I have seen your " sylvan lake,"—
With Nimrod soul have hunted there,
And hoped the timid deer to take,
But often fear'd 'twould be a bear.

" Your sylvan lake,"—yes, let me dream,
And 'mid its shades the past recall,—
The red man's whoop, the eagle's scream,
The grey wolf's bark, the Dutchman's yawl.

And let me see **again let loose**
That essence strong, of soot and whey,—
The spirit of potato juice :—
Pure Aquavita, Uisgebetha !

That flew around in tuns and butts,
The heralds of a stormy night,
And played Old Harry with our guts,
The sure pre-*curse*-ors of a fight.

The soul of every logging bee,
The monarch of **an** ancient fair,
That never **knew the great** N.P.,
But revell'd freely everywhere !

That watched around our natal bed,
And followed through our youthful day,
To see us christen'd, woo'd and wed,
And shrouded too, and packed away.

All this around your sylvan lake
Has had its day and passed, but why
Should mem'ry the dark scenes awake ?
Sweet poet of the lake, good-bye !

MINE AND THINE.

You and yours, and I and mine,
This is how we must divide;
It was always so, in fine,
Each must for himself decide.

We are pilgrims by the way,
Picking up the crumbs that fall;
Strive or struggle as we may,
Fate or fortune rules it all!

Spite of reason, brainless fools
Strut in purple, gather gold;
Wisdom, treasured from the schools,
Coatless, shivers in the cold!

You have equipages and state,
Wealth, and lands, and marble hall;
I a cottage at your gate,
Coldly pitch'd without the wall.

You have fountain, park and bower—
All you wish, and all you will;
I have just the summer shower
That comes down the pools to fill.

You may wander, stray or roam
Over land and over sea;
I must guard my little home,
It is all in all to me.

Yours are mountains high and chill,
Where but eagles only soar;
Sunshine, o'er a gentle hill,
Falls around my cottage door.

Yours are rivers, deep and **wide,**
Bearing treasures to the sea;
Just a rill from mountain side
Sings its evening song to me!

You have someone that you love,
She has diamonds in her hair;
She may frail or fickle prove—
Take her, keep her, I don't care.

I have just a little maid,
Silken tresses, eyes **of blue;**
She can love, I, not **afraid,**
Love me always, she **is true!**

Yours has pedigree and pride,
Quite **a** tall and stately dame;
This, and beauty, much, beside;
Vain and heartless, all **the** same.

Mine has wealth of lineage small,
Wayside flower, a blessing sent;
Scarce ambition **to** be tall—
But I love her, she's content!

I must sweat, and I must toil,
Earn the bread my loved ones eat;
What I owe but to the soil,
Makes partaking twice as sweet!

You may dine on sumptuous fare—
Quaff the wine from vintage old;
Still you only get your share,
If life, and hope, and blood, are cold!

Things are better than they seem—
Blessings not so blindly sent,
Joys we long for prove a dream,
Highest riches, just content.

Thus we journey by the way,
Care we how the die is cast;
Mine and thine are for a day,
We must leave them all at last.

TO SANDY McSNAOISEAN.

(*On the Agricultural Commission.*)

Come Sandy, my man,
Spare an hour gin ye can,
Fra your silly bit haverin' stories;
I'm just comin' back,
To hae a bit crack,
About thae auld reprobate Tories.

I hope ye're a' weel,
In storehouse and creel;
Warm cled, neither hungry nor thirsty;
Good paying returns
Frae ye're Scott Act concerns,
For yersel', the bairnies, and Chirsty.

It's a sennight or mair,
Sin' ye felt raither sair,
Fra the dandin ye're honor cam under;
I think ye fan faut,
Wi' the—what do ye ca'-'t,—
The style or the *double en tendre*!

The crude architect
Was far frae correct,
The Doric was only pretence;
Weel, change we the rule,
Try some ither schule,
Suppose we tak' Composite next.

The pairt I thought true,
Ye thought ower blue,
But often the truth will offend;
Till the lamp cease **to burn,**
Ye still may return,
So just be admonished and mend.

In your reformation,
Ye'll ha'e this consolation,
Ye'll come to receive it in time,—
That truth, when in prose,
Is a gye bitter dose,
But easier swallow'd in rhyme.

Noo, if in my sang
I've din ye a wrang,
Ye needna tak refuge in cant;

For ye ken weel yersel',
What I needna tell,—
That nobody thinks *ye* a saunt.

So noo gin ye're ready,
My auld, snuffin' daddie,
Ye'll ablins be scribe o' the pack ;
Our subject's Protection,
Maybe neest election,
It winna abide the attack.

Noo there's just one condition,
Afore the Commission
Sits doon to its multiplex scheme ;—
Ye're no constituted,
Not enough evoluted,
To grasp so expansive a theme.

But wi' some assistance,
Gin ye mak na resistance,
We'll ablins get over the work.
We'll tak it *verbatim*,
And then *seriatim*,
Frae yer sel to the schemes o' the kirk.

First, that long reprobation
Of endless duration,
That frightened us when we were boys
Frae the card we omit,
Till the fire nor the pit,
Can model nor limit our joys.

But leavin' our kirks,
There's our stots and our stirks,
Oor barley, oor bullocks, an' woo.
They a' **need** defendin',
There's nae use pretendin',
We'll soon hae' to fecht for **it noo** !

We're a' gaun to ruin,
An' waur things are brooin',
Domestic **disunion's in store** ;
For burglars and tramps,
An' blacklegs an' scamps,
Still land, duty free, on oor shore.

There's our shops an' our smiddies,
Fill'd wi' thae foreign **boddies,**
An' oor sons sent adrift every one ;
To increase population,
Wi' oot immigration,
Is the favorite scheme o' Sir J——n.

But ther'il no be a movement,
Toward ony improvement,
Till the Grit usurpation is o'er,
An' **the country is** waiting,
Wi' hope unabating,
To see them pack'd out at the **door.**

Though there's aye some objection,
To a' our perfection,
Some failing, some fleck, or some flaw,—

The laddie the wisest,
The lassie the nicest,
Hae something were better awa'.

So that auld dirty scandal,
Has no lost the handle,
It's **no just so musty and stale**;
An' that fund that they bilket,
An' that coo that they **milket**,
Has no lost the horns nor the *tale*.

An' ye ken weel the French
Were the head and the hench
O' **John** in his golden regime;
An' our cry, Rep. by Pop.,
In the auld Union Shop,
Is no just forgot like a dream.

Sae **we** know very well
Ye wad barter an' sell
Our interests an' rights every one;
For whate'er ye may say
In adversity's day,
Prosperity perjures your man!

For **the** pledges he makes,
His necessity breaks,
Be the pledges themselves right or wrang;
They'll no stan' an hour,
If his place or his power,
'Gainst his troth in the balance sud hang.

There's thac Maritime holes,
  Wi' their codfish an' coals,
We ken baith their threats an' alarms;
  Gin they grin at protection,
  We'll split the connection,
Or try the auld dose,—*better terms!*

Though a duty on coals,
  A sma' circle consoles;
Cauld noses it gies to the rest;
  An' a duty on flour
  Wud stir up a stour
On coals! 'twinna do in the West.

Then there's thac Montrealers,
  An' French lumber haulers,
They hae baith a stomach an' mou;
  Perhaps on reflection,
  They'll find in Protection,
Less promise for them than for you!

They're loyal enough,
  An' a' that kin' o' stuff,
But they ken a' this bosh very weel;
  So I doubt a' the mair
  If their loyalty bear
Twa shillins a pock on their meal!

Their subject in chief,
  Is class, bannocks an' beef,—
Protection,—a farce they deride;

But your pigs an' your stots,
They care na twa groats,
Whether you or the Yankees provide.

Then that souter body,
Wha' deals aye in shoddy,
But warks for the guid o' our *soles* ,
He wants leather free,
An' shoon ! no, not he,
He gruntles an' grieves if he tholes.

Then the tanner wud rather
Draw steel against leather
Than hinder raw hides comin' in,
So the souter an' he,
Though they canna agree,
They're baith o' them death against shoon.

But, Sandy, ye see,
It just suits you an' me,
Gin the bairns hae their taes in the snaw ;
So we'll no just agree,
O' the warl's broose an' brie,
That ane sud hae nane or hae a'.

Still, let one seize the booty,
An' the mass pay the duty,
That's a' that is meant by your cry ;
Yet to say that free trade
Gies the poor claes an' bread,
Is treason o' deadliest dye !

MORNING.

I WOKE in sunny Eastern clime,
Where, or how distant, none can tell;
With birds 'twas happy mating time,
And life and joy in bower and dell.

O'er head, the April skies were blue,
And through the air the breath of Spring;
And in a grove, where violets grew,
I know I heard a robin sing.

Rich fragrance floated on the breeze,
And bud and flower love whispering were;
Low voices murmured through the trees,
That somehow taught me God was there!

And songs returned of other lands,
Where I had wandered long ago,
Like sighing wavelets on the sands,
Or mem'ry's music, soft and low.

But syrens wooed my heart away,
Youth's days were o'er, and boyhood fled;
In all that flowery vale of May,
I found not where to lay my head.

I wandered forth at dawn of day,
To climb ambition's flowery hill;
'Twas just a league or two away,—
At evening I was climbing still.

I sought the summit, but the night
O'ercast with clouds my guiding star,
And morn found other hills in sight,
As fair with promise, but as far !

Wan pilgrims resting by the way,
With hands uplifted to the hill,
Lured by the promise of life's May,
Pursued that paling phantom still.

They knew that just that summit o'er,
Was ocean wide, with waters blue,—
That when their footsteps reached its shore,
No other hills would rise to view.

I passed the summit, reached the shore,
But onward moved the guiding star,
And when I deemed the struggle o'er,
Rose higher, fairer hills afar.

Then thought I : Mortal, wherefore toil ?
What gain in all this weary strife ?
Rest from ambition's drunken broil,
And gather in the sweets of life.

Then builded I a palace fair,
The dream of many longing years;
But when at eve I rested there,
I know my eyes were dim with tears.

I planted garden, grove and bower,
And watched for sunshine, shower and dew ;
And longed for Autumn's crowning hour,
But not the flowers I planted grew.

Oh! blot me out all mem'ry's store,
Of strife and struggle, failure, pain,
And bring me boyhood's dreams once more,
Of faith and hope in life again!

FAREWELL, GENTLE MUSE.

FAREWELL, gentle Muse, 'tis the time we should sever,
The dark shades of winter descend o'er the plain;
But O! though we part it shall not be forever,
The first breath of spring shall unite us again!
When May fills the grove with song and commotion,
Spreads flowers o'er the hill, and awakens the bee;
When swallows return from their homes, 'yond the ocean,
Then shalt thou come back, gentle Muse, unto me.

Though far from thine own native hills thou must wander,
And here for a season self-banishment bear;
Though where thou must come boasts not greatness nor
     grandeur,
And I who await thee unworthy thy care.
Yet come, though our song be but broken in measure,
Untuned to the eloquent cadence of art,
It still may awaken the warm glow of pleasure,
If love be our theme, and our lyre be the heart.

Long, long have you followed through sunshine and
     shadow,
And gave to my longings a voice and a tongue,—
Changed the sigh of the pine, and the notes of the meadow,
The one into worship, the other to song.

Oh give me one hour of the glow and the glory,
The shimmer of brightness that hung on the hill,
When youth took the highway to learn life's sad story,
With hope the enchantress deluding me still !

Then come, draw thy wild mountain garment about thee,
We journey together while life may remain ;
To me 'twere bereavement and darkness without thee,
And soon comes the morn when we meet not again.
But adieu ! hie thee hence ere the rude blast of winter
O'ertake thee too early and shrivel thy wing ;—
Lest haply, again thou mayest not venture
So far o'er the ocean, e'en if it were spring !